BLUEGRASS SECURITY

FINISH *Line*

USA TODAY BESTSELLING AUTHOR

PJ FIALA

I've had so many wonderful people come into my life, and I want you all to know how much I appreciate you. From each and every reader who takes the time out of their day to read my stories and leave reviews, thank you.

My beta readers, Anita, Barbara, and Teresa; ladies, thank you so very much for your suggestions, praise, and time.

Thank you to my proofreader, Sara - I appreciate you.

To my family, my greatest blessing and unwavering support system. Your love, encouragement, and sacrifices have made this dream possible.

And to my husband and best friend, Gene—thank you for standing beside me every step of the way. Your belief in me, your patience, and your love are the foundation of everything I do. Words will never be enough to express how much you mean to me, but I will spend my life showing you.

***

To our veterans and all those currently serving in the armed forces, police, fire departments, and as EMTs—your courage, dedication, and sacrifices do not go unnoticed. Thank you for *your unwavering commitment to protecting and serving. It is with heartfelt gratitude and deep respect that I honor you here. You are the true heroes, and your contributions inspire every word on these pages.*

DESCRIPTION

Enjoy this small-town steamy romantic suspense series by USA Today bestselling author PJ Fiala.

One retired military officer.

Plus one sassy detective.

Equals a race for answers and desire.

Building the Bluegrass Security business in a small town is the perfect opportunity for Sam "Mac" McKenzie to settle down and plant his roots once and for all. But a one-night-stand with a beautiful and feisty detective leads him to an investigation that changes everything.

Bourbon-loving Stevie Jorgenson loves a hot case--and a hot man. But her latest case hits a little too close to home. With prize-winning horses ending up dead days before the Kentucky Derby, Stevie knows she has to act fast. Enlisting the help of the sexy and rugged security investigator is her only option. Sparks fly while they unearth answers they never expected. As the finish line nears, are

Stevie and Mac racing for more than they ever bargained for?

Finish Line is the second novel in the Bluegrass Security Romance Series, although all books in the Bluegrass world can be read as standalones. A steamy romantic story with a guaranteed happily ever after, it does have some strong language and exciting sexy times. Enjoy Mac and Stevie!

Looking for stories filled with heart-pounding suspense, steamy romance, and unforgettable characters? Sign up for my newsletter and get a **FREE book** to dive into right away!

It's easy: 1 Sign up below. 2 Confirm your email (we like to keep things legit and bot-free 😉). 3 Start enjoying your free read and exclusive updates, sneak peeks, and special offers!

📚 Love awaits—don't miss your chance to join the adventure!

https://www.pjfiala.com/subscribe/

1

Stevie Jorgenson leaned against the bar stool, hiking her heel up behind her to hang on the metal rung. She'd been here at the Brass Rail Saloon, for the better part of an hour—it was her relaxation. She came in after her day was done, had a couple of bourbons, beat a few guys at pool and strutted home—hopefully with a few extra dollars in her pocket. She preferred playing for a buck and a drink, which usually meant she drank for free and made a little money.

Picking up the drink from the oak-covered ledge next to her, she sipped the fiery bourbon and closed her eyes as the warmth slid down her throat and settled low in her belly. Man, she loved that feeling, it made her feel alive.

Laughter erupted across the bar, boots stamped on the scarred wood floor, and the oak door slammed. A slow smile slid across her face. The place was finally filling up, which meant she'd be shooting some pool soon. She eyed the small group that had walked in—four men and a woman. They pulled up to a tall table on the other side of the half wall where she stood. She didn't recognize these folks, which wasn't unusual this time of year; the Derby brought in loads of new faces. The group was clearly friends as they jovially teased and taunted each other while their drinks were served. She kind of envied that. She had a couple of close friends, but these days they didn't get together much. Toni had gotten married about ten years ago and had three adorable—but very busy—children. She was running from dance class to band practice to baseball and back around again. They spoke on the phone often and about once a quarter they managed a night out when Toni's husband, Al, managed to wrangle the kids to give her some girl time.

The woman had a small build, long dark hair and dark eyes, and was exotic in a wholesome sort of way. Tomboyish. She wore jeans, a long deep blue T-shirt that hugged her slight curves and she wore what looked like Army boots. She had a colorful full-sleeve tattoo on her right arm of red roses. It was stunning.

One of the men seemed to be her man as he hung his arm around her shoulders in more than a casual way. His sandy brown hair was laced with silver, and he had a deep scar on his forearm. Then he leaned in and kissed her, and the way they looked into each other's eyes afterward made Stevie's stomach clench just a bit. She sipped the warm amber liquid in her glass and let the fire settle the churning.

A large blond man, easily six foot four or five and broad as a barn, seemed almost shy as he stood with the group, but yet, held himself slightly aloof. His hair curled at the collar and was long around the ears. He was either growing it out or sorely in need of a cut. His blue eyes held intelligence but he seemed a bit unsure of himself.

The smaller man of the group wore short, cropped blond hair and had the most stunning blue eyes she'd ever seen. His easy laugh and jolly disposition made her smile, and she watched with rapt attention as he teased the other man in the group. Now that one—mmm. He was fine. Mighty fine.

Six foot two or so with dark, sultry eyes and hair. Silver strands glinted in the light when he turned his head. He jovially nudged the shorter man with his elbow and laughed. Oh my! His full lips lifted and the dimples popped out. On both sides. Yowza! He glanced her way and the look he laid on her damn near melted her panties. Holy hell! He nodded, then picked up his drink, and she couldn't stop watching his Adam's apple bob as he swallowed the amber liquid—the same color as hers, incidentally—in his glass. He probably drove a big-ass pickup truck and a motorcycle. He'd look killer driving either.

"Another one, Stevie?" the bubbly waitress, oddly named Schmoo, loudly chirped.

She turned to her right and assessed Schmoo. She had bright, curly-red hair and freckles strewn across her nose and cheeks. She wore bib overall shorts and white socks pushed down to the top of her brown, construction-type boots. The younger woman looked twelve; but, of course, she had to be older to serve alcohol, but damned if you could tell.

"Yep. Why is everyone so late getting here today?"

Schmoo looked around as if she'd just noticed the bar was emptier than usual.

"Carnival pulled in a while ago, so you know..." She shrugged her shoulders. "Folks love to go gawk at the carnies. They'll be around soon."

Schmoo strutted away as if she were a dancer, light on her feet—even in boots.

Stevie smiled as she watched the red curls bouncing about her head. That girl could put you in a good mood just looking at her.

"You shooting or just holding up the wall?"

Before she could grasp the situation, her nipples puckered to sharp points, and moisture gathered between her legs. She turned to see the tall, dark drink of water standing in her space, shadowing her from the light. He smelled heavenly, like expensive aftershave and the combination of the aroma and the deep, slow, sultry voice rose the gooseflesh on her arms.

She swallowed to moisten her throat. Then swallowed again, because just being this close to him did funny things to her. "Shootin'. For a buck and a drink. Last pocket," she managed to say, proud of herself for not stammering.

He nodded once and bent to slide his four quarters into the pool table coin slot. Pushing in and releasing, the loud crack of balls hitting the rails and rolling toward the end signaled it was playtime. She watched as his muscles straining under the gray T-shirt bunched and flattened as he gracefully pulled the pool balls from their landing place and laid them into the triangle. He stood and rearranged the balls sorting the solids from the stripes and bunching them together with his hands. She couldn't stop looking at the way his thick, long fingers danced across the balls.

He turned and caught her gaze with his, and the burning in her stomach had nothing to do with the bourbon this time. The man was positively smoldering. She walked to the other end of the pool table, as much to break as to put some space between her and the dark, mysterious man breathing the same air as she. She leaned down, eyed her mark and cracked the cue with the white ball, sending the colorful balls in all directions, but not dropping anything into a pocket. Shit.

She nodded to him. He smirked then proceeded to bend over the table and sink three balls into various pockets. All solids. The sting of not getting the first ball in was tempered by the sight of his fine ass as he smoothly draped his form over the table. She'd bring this one to his knees later when she stripped for him and proceeded to have her way with his body. Yep, that was her new plan now. Pool didn't hold the same appeal anymore. She'd been celibate for far too long now, and it was time to have a little fun. She sent up a silent prayer, Thank you, Lord, for bringing someone interesting into Bourbonville.

The game continued, mostly in silence, unless one or the other of them needed to call a pocket. Their subtle mating dance, preening and stretching before each other, was the only other thing going on in the room. Her attention was constantly diverted from her game as she watched his panther-like movements stalk the table and sink each ball in one by one. He always watched the exits as he stood and before he bent, a quick glance telling her he was probably military or ex-military. Always vigilant.

His scent floated over her once more as he walked past, leaned down, and sunk the eight ball into the last pocket. He laid his cue on the table and slowly turned to her as he crooned, "I'll take bourbon – Ethan's new blend."

Their eyes met, and the heat climbed her body, staining her cheeks as a shiver ran amok to the tips of her toes. Damn. He wore a slight smile on his face as his dark eyes raked over her face and her breasts before landing on her lips. The intensity of his stare made her nipples pucker again, and her breath came in spurts. His expensive-smelling cologne floated over her, and she had a hard time moving. She wanted to squeeze her thighs closed, but that would be obvious. Then he spoke, and the deep, rich tone damn near made her lose it.

"Sam. My friends call me Mac." He held his hand out to her, and it took her a few moments to come back to earth.

"Stevie. My friends call me Stevie." Her hand grasped his and her fingers wrapped around his firmly, pumping twice before stopping. The heat of his hand ran up her arm, and she shivered.

"So, Stevie isn't short for anything?" he teased. A slow smile slid across his handsome face. His deep brown eyes twinkled in the dim light of the poolroom.

Her heartbeat raced, and the air left her lungs when she heard his low chuckle.

"Yes." Her voice cracked. She swallowed and tried again. "Stephanie."

He nodded his head once, never looking away from her, then released her hand. The loss left her wanting more. His gaze slid down her body, and it felt like the hot lick of a tongue. When his eyes made the trip back to hers, he leaned against the pool table, resting his fine ass on the edge, and crossed his arms over his chest.

She managed a smile with her trembling lips and nodded once as she found a way to make her feet move toward the bar to buy his drink.

Well fuck me, he thought as her hand wrapped around his, her soft fingers firmly grasping his. The difference in size was amazing, and the soft texture of her skin felt like a satin glove over his hand. The crisp blue of her eyes reminded him of the summer sky—clear and exciting. The whites of her eyes were bright, with no telltale signs of sleep loss or sitting at a computer all day. Watching her dip and stretch that sultry body over the table had him ducking behind a tall bar top table more than once, especially when she leaned over toward him and her blue, button-up blouse showed him the sexy cleavage of her voluptuous breasts. When he drew close to her, the scent of peaches filled his nostrils and made him think of clean and wholesome. But the way she looked at him was anything but wholesome. And he imagined he looked at her the same way.

He sat on the edge of the pool table and watched the fine sway of her ass as she walked to the bar, pulling money from her back pocket as she made her way across the scarred wooden floor. She chatted with the bartender, Ethan Hastings, one of the bar's owners, turned to lock eyes with him, then turned away again. Ethan chuckled, his blue eyes darting around the room as he poured drinks—never missing a beat. Stevie picked up the two glasses of Bourbon and walked toward him, her ample breasts swaying slightly.

Their fingers brushed as he took his drink from her hand, and her pupils grew making her baby blues deepen. Her mouth opened and he thought he detected a sigh. Perfect! He hadn't been laid since he'd rolled into this town three months ago—dry spell over.

He held his glass up, "Salud," then tapped it to hers and sipped.

He watched over the rim as she drank down a healthy mouthful, her eyes slid closed, and a soft smile graced her face. When her eyes opened she looked straight into his; her expression changed from serene to humorous as her smile widened.

"I love feeling the warm slide," she admitted. The quality of her voice reminded him of Kathleen Turner—low and smoldering.

Ah, yes, his cue. He leaned forward and whispered, "I've got another warm slide I think you'll enjoy just as much." This time there was no mistaking the shiver that slithered down her body, his eyes instantly slid to her breasts, and he saw the peaked nipples slightly through her bra. She was going to be fun.

Her voice deepened. "I'll bet you do," she husked. "I think you'll enjoy it just as much as I will."

His nostrils flared, and he breathed in deeply, inhaling the peachy scent and quickly growing impatient. "Let's go."

Her smile widened. She kicked back the remaining spirits and gracefully set her glass on the half wall. Her brows raised as she stared into his. A slow smile spread across her face, mocking him, maybe daring him. He didn't need more than that. He slammed back his drink, set his empty glass next to hers, then glanced back at his friends and waved. Stevie took his hand in hers and led him through the poolroom and down the short hallway to the back door. Stepping from the dark bar into the late afternoon sunlight caused him to blink. He briefly glanced around and saw no vehicles in sight, the back lot nothing more than enough space for three cars, at most, and the dumpster area. The dark wood siding would need a coat of paint in the next year or so, but the air smelled oddly fresh—like laundry detergent.

He eagerly followed without speaking, his need growing as he hungrily watched her ass moving with each step, hampering the long strides he wanted to take to anywhere, so he could slide into her. She glanced back once, her blonde hair swishing over her shoulders, a sexy smile opening her lips. Her hand squeezed his and tugged him forward as if she were more eager than he. Highly unlikely.

They crossed the alley, their footsteps crunching on the gravel. The late afternoon sun still brightened the sky, and the halo that formed around her head caused him to chuckle.

She looked back, "What are you laughing at?"

He shook his head. "The sun cast a halo around your head."

She laughed, and it was akin to a perfect melody. His stomach twisted. "Honey, I'm no angel," she silkily replied, and he stumbled.

She giggled and tugged harder. Reaching into her front pocket, she pulled out a key attached to a little horseshoe. She held it up for him to see then pointed to an upstairs apartment, a little wooden deck protruding from the red brick building. She unlocked a door and stepped inside. "Turn the lock behind you please." She let go of his hand as she climbed the stairs. Nice view.

He turned, twisted the lock and followed just far enough behind that her derriere was directly in front of his face. The old wooden steps creaked and groaned as his weight moved from one to the next, the little enclosed staircase lit only by the windows situated every fourth step or so. No decorations brightened the area; nothing made it feel like a home.

She unlocked the door at the top of the steps and stepped into the apartment. He was pleasantly surprised as he entered behind her. The light tan walls were decorated with pictures of beautiful purebred horses; one of them running along a fence line, three professionally framed photos of horses standing at the grandstand, a ring of roses slung around their necks, their nostrils flared as the pride in their eyes gleamed back at him. She set her key on the oak table, and he couldn't help but notice the crystals embedded into the horseshoe. Her apartment smelled like fresh laundry soap and fabric softener.

"You need something to drink?" she silkily asked.

He turned to her and watched as she slowly unbuttoned her blouse. He was mesmerized by her nimble fingers, and she made short work of each one. "No," was all he could manage.

He pulled his gray T-shirt from his jeans and swiftly pulled it over his head. Draping it over the back of one of the upholstered kitchen chairs, he leaned down and untied his work boots, watching as she did the same. She finished first and pushed her boots toward the wall under the picture of a sprawling ranch surrounded by horses.

Standing, she unhooked her bra, a slow sexy smile gracing her face. She let it fall to her hands, then slowly turned and walked to a door and disappeared into another room. Damn.

He fumbled with his boot laces, finished pulling them from his feet, shoved his socks into his boots and followed the sexy siren calling him from the other room. His motor was revved to a hundred miles per hour.

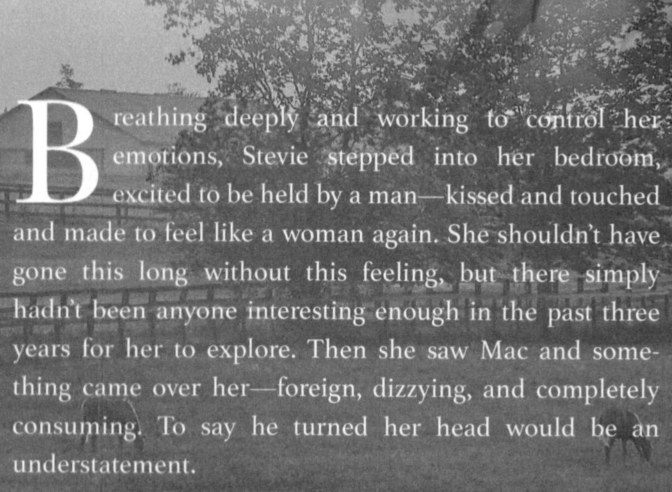

2

Breathing deeply and working to control her emotions, Stevie stepped into her bedroom, excited to be held by a man—kissed and touched and made to feel like a woman again. She shouldn't have gone this long without this feeling, but there simply hadn't been anyone interesting enough in the past three years for her to explore. Then she saw Mac and something came over her—foreign, dizzying, and completely consuming. To say he turned her head would be an understatement.

She unzipped her tan dress pants and slid them over her hips. She stepped from the pooled fabric on the floor and bent to pick them up, keeping an ear turned toward the kitchen. She heard his pants hit the floor and his footsteps coming toward her. The gooseflesh that rose on her arms at the sound of his voice as he stepped into her bedroom surprised her again.

"You are a sexy woman, Stevie," he rumbled as he took the three steps to reach her. His warm, calloused hands gripped her shoulders and pulled her into his nearly naked body. The ridges and shadows made by the abs he sported and the dusting of dark hair across his chest gave her a thrill she'd barely experienced before. She placed her hands on his chest and ran them down each of the ridges until she reached the waistband of his briefs. She toyed with the waistband sliding her fingers partially under and sliding them around his waist to the back. She stood shorter than he, her mouth directly in front of his nipples. She licked her lips and sucked one into her mouth, flicking her tongue over the taut rosebud. He huffed out a groan, and she smiled against his chest. His fingers tightened on her shoulders, and she moved to the other little peak, laving it with her tongue before sucking it into her mouth. Her hands sought his manhood, and she was not disappointed at what she found. Wrapping her fingers around his firm length, she heard his sharp intake of breath, and she allowed her hand to squeeze firmly as she pumped him, roving her thumb over the head before gliding down to his base, the curls tickling her fingers.

He pulled her away from him, and she sought his gaze. Those dark orbs stared into hers and the color darkened further. His full kissable lips softly pushed out to the most adorable pout. Silver strands glistened from his dark hair, the waning sunlight highlighting each one. Sexy.

He leaned down and softly pressed his lips to hers and her knees weakened. His arms wrapped around her body, pulling her fully to him, all his hard ridges and planes fitting to her body in the most delicious way. When his tongue slid along hers, the hint of bourbon filled her senses as his warmth seeped into her skin. His body felt sturdy and strong and so very male.

He began walking her backward till her legs hit the bed and he slowly bent them till she lay down, he held himself just above her. Her hands sought his skin, needing the connection, enjoying the heat and the shiver of his skin below her fingers. His breathing grew shallow, and a small smile played upon her lips as she enjoyed eliciting a response from him. It made her feel powerful in a way. She looked up and locked eyes with him, unable to look away. Her heart beat so fast it mimicked the horse hooves pounding the dirt track as they raced to the finish. She swallowed to moisten her parched throat and slowly raised her legs and wrapped them around the back of his legs.

He slowly leaned down and pressed his lips to hers commanding her lips, tongue, even her very breath. The bed dipped as he leaned to one side slightly and pushed his briefs down with one hand. She reached down to assist as the heat rose up her body. Her fingers shook as she pushed the offending fabric from his hips. When she could reach no more, she used her toes to slide them to the floor. Their breathing increased, and he pulled away just long enough to pull her panties down in one swift tug, then he was on her again, his lips dominating hers.

He kissed his way down her neck, then to her ear. His voice was gravelly when he asked, "Fast or slow?"

"Fast. Now," she managed between kissing him and nipping him with her teeth. His scent was spicy, the aroma filling the air as his skin heated.

"Good answer," he breathed as he lifted himself slightly, taking his cock in his hand and directing it into her wetness. As he slowly pushed himself into her, she mewled at the feeling of being filled, his warm hardness massaging her from the inside.

He groaned as he seated himself fully then pulled out to plunge in again. His pace increased, and she tilted her hips to receive him. Their union consumed them both, each racing toward the final moment of ecstasy. The room grew warm. The bed under her rocked, and she hung on to his body, pulling him toward her so she could feel the firmness against her. He rotated his hips, and she stiffened as her orgasm rolled over her. She cried out something unintelligible as he picked up his pace catching up to her. His deep groan as he plunged into her once more and held himself still, rent the air.

She relaxed back into the mattress and allowed her arms to fall to her sides. He dipped his head to the bed, his breathing coming in short bursts.

After a few moments, he rolled over and lay beside her, both staring at the ceiling. Now what? She'd never done anything like this before; she was out of her element.

He stared at the ceiling, his body still reeling from their encounter. It had been a while for him, but damn it, that was simply fantastic. Her body fit his in every way. Her intoxicating taste and feel was simply perfect. But, he had to be real, she probably did this all the time. She didn't bat an eye when he said, "Let's go." Easy walk across the alley and in mere minutes he was in her. He wasn't going to get involved with someone who'd end up cheating on him in the end. Been there. Done that.

He sat up and ran his hands through his hair, stood, picked his briefs up, and easily stepped into them. He stepped out into the kitchen and gathered his clothing and redressed quickly. He sat in a kitchen chair to pull on his boots when she stepped into the room wearing cutoff denim shorts and a yellow tank top without a bra. Damn. Her ample breasts easily moved when she walked and he found it nearly impossible to look anywhere else. She leaned against the counter and watched him as he finished lacing his boots.

He stood, walked to her and kissed her lightly on the lips. "See ya around?"

She scrunched her face slightly. "Sure." She crossed her arms, and he took that as a protective sign.

He shrugged. "Gotta get home and feed my pup."

Her face brightened. "What kind of puppy do you have?"

He relaxed and answered. "A Belgian Malinois. A cousin to the German Shepard. He's two now, full of energy, and needs to be exercised. He's my baby in a way."

She visibly stiffened and tightened her arms around her middle. She made no move toward him, so he shrugged slightly and stepped toward the door, opened it, and glanced back at her. "It was nice meeting you, Stevie."

He hurried down the steps, his thoughts in a jumble, his stomach knotted at leaving her, but it appeared she was ready for him to go. It was for the best anyway.

3

Baby. Figures. He was one of those nurturing kind of guys who wanted to have a house full of babies one day. She was glad he'd left so easily; it saved her from having to figure out what now. But, it was a pity. He was the first man in a long time. No, wait, ever, to make her heart pound as it did. Next time she had sex, she'd make sure she didn't wait three years. Yeah, that was it. Abstinence made her think screwy things.

Her phone began playing *Fishin' in the Dark* by Nitty Gritty Dirt Band, her father's ringtone. Typical dad-timing. She picked it up off the counter and swiped the answer icon.

"Hey, Dad, what's up?" She leaned her backside against the cabinets, her left foot perched on top of her right, her free hand combing through her hair, smoothing the tangles which she'd just made. A flush raced up her body at the thought of Mac. Involuntarily she glanced toward the bedroom door.

"Hey, Stevie, I need you to come out here to the ranch. I just had a horse poisoned. The mare that I was hoping to race next year."

Her father's tired voice alerted her. She stood up straight and walked to the bedroom. "How do you know it was poisoned?"

"Doc Burgis was just here." She heard his long exhale, and her heart ached. Unbelievable.

"Dad." She slipped on her boots. "Could it have gotten into something? What poison was used? Has there been anyone strange hanging around?" She clumsily pulled her tank top off.

"Hold on, Stevie. I'll answer all of your questions, but I need to get a few things done, and Dan is just now coming back into the barn. Please come out here."

"Yeah. I'm on my way." She ended the call, slipped on her bra, pulled her tank over her head, grabbed her purse from the brown leather chair in her living room, and headed down the stairs she'd not long ago ascended. That darn flush tinted her cheeks again as she remembered Mac's hands on her, and his scent was still swirling through her brain.

At the bottom of the steps, she opened a side door and entered her garage, which was directly behind the Laundromat at the front of this building. The fabric softeners and laundry soaps used inside always lent a fresh scent to her garage and her apartment upstairs.

She jumped in her Jeep, hit the garage door opener and backed from the building. The ride to her father's ranch was gorgeous on the worst days. The country roads winding out of town led her through the aromas of magnolia floating in the breeze. The green grass in the lawns and fields of the area ranches was a sight to behold. The gracefulness of the horses running and prancing in the fields always made her heart ping for home.

Turning down the blacktop driveway, she drove through the white fenced pastures. On the left, the mares grazed lazily in the early evening sunlight; on the right, the foals —now youngsters—played with each other. The winding driveway turned, and the expanse of Balmoral came into view. The massive brick mansion, inherited from her grandparents and their parents before them, was still held in high regard in Bourbonville, even after the murder of her grandfather at the hands of his insipid second wife. The Georgian, red brick structure, was three stories tall with four thick white columns supporting the upper balcony and enough windows to keep a housekeeper busy for a year. Her family had been here for four generations, farmed this land, raised award-winning thoroughbreds, and won more than a few Derbies. Her legacy. But she didn't want to go into the ranching business; she wanted to be a detective. And she worked hard at it. She'd forsaken all of the family luxuries, worked her way through school, became a police officer, and worked her ass off to make detective.

She maneuvered her Jeep to the left, coming to a stop in front of the barn. The large structure, painted the requisite red and white, wore its fresh paint well. Balmoral was undergoing many renovations under her mother's keen eye. The barn was not left unchanged in that.

She jumped from her vehicle and entered the barn, which was eerily quiet today. The smell of fresh hay greeted her. A few of the barn cats came running to see if she had milk or to get a scratch behind the ears. She patted each one, scurrying them away as she made her way to a far stall where the low voices of her father and Dan, the head ranch hand, could be faintly heard.

"Dad. Dan," she said as she reached the stall, the wooden door open, the two men kneeling down next to a beautiful bay mare, laying in a fresh bed of straw, her breathing labored, her eyes closed. A mournful moan came from the sick beauty, and her dad's eyes welled with tears.

Her dad's sad blue eyes, the mirror of her own, held hers, the thin line his lips formed meant he was working to hold it together. "Not sure if she'll make it," he said softly as he reached for her and hugged her tightly.

Dan stood, his body lean, the smattering of gray streaking through his hair the only telltale signs of his fifty plus years. He held his hand out to her. "Thanks for coming, Stevie. Always nice to see you, but not like this."

She nodded at this man who'd been in her father's employ for many years. "Hi, Dan. Is there anything she could have gotten into?" Her detective radar kicked in.

"Nothing. All of our drugs are locked in the office. The tack is secure, and nothing is out of place or moved. We don't keep pesticides or poisons anywhere near the barn here; they're all out in the back shed. I just came from there, and nothing has been touched." He shook his head and glanced down at the struggling mare. She moaned lightly, and he knelt alongside her and lovingly stroked her neck, crooning soft words to calm her. "We've had the fields cleaned of all harmful vegetation for years, but I do have a ranch hand checking the back pasture to make sure nothing has grown back."

Her dad nodded toward the end of the barn and began walking in that direction. She followed him, glancing around the barn—always pristine and neat—an actual showplace. As they passed the various stalls, twenty in this section of the barn, the other four sections also held twenty in each; horses watched them with interest. The occasional neigh or blowing broke the silence.

Stepping outside in the dusky evening, her dad stopped and turned to her. "I wonder if that son of a bitch Carlson's at it again. We haven't had any problems in years, and now here we go again."

She tilted her head to the side. "Dad, you don't have any proof, do you?"

The silver strands in her dad's sandy hair sparkled in the low light of the day. His normally perfect posture dipped with the weight of losing a possible Derby winner. That's how his business had grown over the years. He rubbed his chin with his fingers, then swiped his hands down his face. "No." He planted his hands on his hips. "But this smacks of his father's former work."

She stepped forward and wrapped her arms around her father's waist and squeezed him. She laid her head on his shoulder and breathed in the familiar scent of his Old Spice aftershave, still present despite his full day of work. Her voice was a bit muffled when she said, "I'll do what I can to figure this out."

4

———

Now that he'd gotten that out of his system, he'd be able to concentrate on work. Nothing like a hot tumble to clear his head. And, Stevie was hot. The moment he'd laid eyes on her his radar was up, and testosterone pumped through his body at the speed of the fastest thoroughbred. But, he couldn't get all wrapped up with her. End of story.

Pulling into his driveway, Ammo shot out of the doggy door and happily bounced around his truck. A genuine smile slid across his face as his furry housemate eagerly awaited his homecoming. Coming to a full stop, he put the truck in park, pulled his keys from the ignition and opened the door to the squealing mass of fur. Leaning down to properly scratch Ammo behind the ears and receive the tongue bath a long absence required, he felt at home—almost.

"Okay, boy, let's go get us something to eat."

His new routine consisted of feeding Ammo, then himself. Then, he'd work out. He was so happy he'd finally turned the back bedroom into his home gym. Bourbonville was a nice little town to live in, but it lacked certain things – a place to work out being just one.

Ham piled high on his whole grain bread and brown mustard squirted on the top was his dinner tonight. He grabbed a beer and headed outside to eat his sandwich and watch Ammo play in the lake in his backyard. It was the reason he bought this house; it was serene and peaceful. After more than twenty-five years in the Army and schlepping from base to base—deployments and the like —having his own place for the first time in his life was what kept him sane as the bullets were flying past his head. Now that he'd purchased his own home and got himself a dog, thinking that would make him happy, it seemed something was still missing. Probably just needed to finish some of the repairs on the house and completely settle in. He'd only been in Kentucky for three months now—not enough time to feel at home.

Setting his empty plate on the table alongside his chaise, he leaned his head back and watched the waning sun's rays glint off the ripples in the water created by the frogs and fish. The golden orb in the sky cast red and gold tones on the water which had given this lake its name – Fire Lake.

He could almost hear a marching cadence in the frog croaks if he listened long enough. A wet ball dropped in his lap, the soft panting from Ammo breaking into his reverie. He picked up the ball and tossed it out into the lake, his black and tan Belgian, running after it, creating a loud splash as he jumped into the water.

His phone rang, and he leaned back to fish it from his pocket.

"Mac."

A soft giggle from the other end made him smile. "Hey, you left in a hurry," one of his partners, Sage, replied.

"Never mind, Sage."

"Just a friendly reminder that you have to be at the Carlson ranch tomorrow. Big operation, needs cameras, full-blown security, perimeter surveillance, the works."

He whistled. "I remember; it's why we were celebrating."

Sage giggled again. "Yep. It's our third big security job on one of the ranches in the area, and this one didn't come from the Pages, so that's progress. We're so excited."

Sam watched Ammo run toward him, lime green ball in his mouth, the water flying in all directions from his coat mimicked glitter dancing in the air as the sun's last rays glinted off the droplets.

"I'll be in early to gather my equipment and get on out there. Who's helping me, Chuck or Dirks?"

"Chuck will be here for you. See you in the morning."

The morning sun rose at 6:58 a.m., but he'd been awake for almost two hours by then. Excitement coursed through his veins at the good fortune shining down on Bluegrass Security. They'd done their homework—he and his first partner, Dirks. They had a friend who came from money and who was instrumental in getting them set up. Charles Page spread the word among the ranchers in the area and further threw his support behind them by being their first big client. His fellow ranchers had formed an association which sponsored new businesses, offered business advice to their clients, and kept the riffraff out of the area.

After filling Ammo's water and food dishes, he left his place feeling refreshed and positive. He arrived at the Bluegrass Security office before anyone else. It still thrilled him to walk into the office. The two-story brick building, while nondescript on the outside, it was anything but on the inside. The first floor held their supply room in the back, shelves of security cameras, wire spools, controllers and brackets, locked up tight.

At the front and entering from the street, it looked like any other office in small town America. The walls were painted a coral tone, which the men all hated but Sage insisted was important. The seating area for customers and prospective clients coming in held cushioned swivel chairs and a large counter with a desk behind it where Regina, their receptionist, sat.

Regina was a force to be reckoned with. Tall, svelte and striking, her mocha skin and short cropped hair gave her the appearance of someone's eye candy. But, she was former Army, badass, and no one would get past her who wasn't supposed to. She was perfect for them. Besides being a single mother and not interested in performing the work they did, she'd needed a job and loved the idea of Bluegrass Security, so that piece of the puzzle fit for them.

The second floor was operation central. Eight desks sat in three rows, each supporting three large computer monitors and very little else. Keyboards were hidden in trays that slid under the desktops. Only two employees were manning the desks overnight, but as they grew, there was room for more.

He nodded to the employees and entered the office that he and Dirks shared. After looking over the job order that Levi had written up, he gathered the supplies they'd need for their job today. Packing the final load into the back of his pickup, he walked through the back door of the office to the aroma of freshly brewing coffee.

"Morning, Levi; I see you got an early start."

Sage was the brightest spot in this office. She always had a smile on her petite face and a no-nonsense attitude to boot. "Morning. Yep, wanted to get started on the Carlson ranch and make a good impression."

Levi Jacobson, another of the four partners of Bluegrass Security and Sage's significant other, limped into the front door of the office, a scowl on his face.

Mac nodded at his friend. "Sore today?"

The grimace on Levi's face grew. "Out of pills." He limped to the coffee station, leaned over to kiss Sage, and crossed his arms.

Sage smiled. "You should have said something when you took the last one, Levi. I'll run to the drugstore now and pick up your prescription before work has us hopping."

She hurried to the door, her long dark hair tied in its usual tail at her nape and bounded out with her usual unlimited energy.

Mac tucked the paperwork for the job into his briefcase, poured a cup of coffee for himself and his friend and handed Levi his. Levi caught his gaze, and though his jaw was tight, he managed to tease. "How'd things work out for you last night? Did you even talk to the little hottie before you banged her?"

Mac froze and stared at his longtime friend. For some reason, even though over the years they'd pick at each other often just like this, it pissed him off today.

"Don't be crude just because your leg hurts, Levi."

That brought a faint smile to Levi's face. "She got to you?"

"No, of course not. I just ... it's not ..." He picked up his briefcase with a huff. "I don't want to talk about it."

He began walking to the back door when it opened, and Chuck walked in. "Mornin'."

Chuck was a massive man-child—always jovial and happy and the size of a small truck. His twinkling blue eyes always held humor and good nature, and he always seemed to need a haircut. It was hard not to be in a good mood around the big-ass farm boy. "Mornin' Chuck. I'll be in the truck. I've got it loaded and ready to go."

The smile slipped from Chuck's round face. "Okay." He turned to follow him out the door. "See ya, Levi," he called out before closing the door behind him. Tossing his case into the back seat and climbing into the driver's seat, he sipped his coffee and turned the key in the ignition. A bit of coffee spilled onto his hand as the truck dipped under Chuck's weight.

The ride to the Carlson ranch was serene. Chuck was quiet most of the trip but couldn't control himself as they turned down the long curved drive of the ranch. The expanse of green pasture in front of the white house was picture perfect. Though the fences needed a coat of paint, the wood was solid. A tractor leisurely made its way across a back field, the fresh hay it cut attracting flocks of birds eager for fresh nesting materials. "I've never seen so many barns painted black in my life. What's the deal with that?" Chuck asked.

A trainer walked a horse from one paddock to another as Mac parked the truck in front of the black barn.

"I asked that when I first arrived. It seems it was a trend—or is one—and it just stuck."

They began unloading the truck and arranging their equipment in the order they'd need it. The ranch owner, Evanston Carlson, greeted them. "Morning. Nice to see you here bright and early."

"Yes, sir." Mac shook hands with the rotund man. Carlson wore a thick mustache, waxed at the ends to form the faintest hint of a curl. That look went out with the thirties, but Evanston Carlson seemed not to notice.

"I've heard a Bay was poisoned over at Balmoral and I can't afford to have that happen here. So, I want the works as I told your employer yesterday."

"Partner." Mac placed his hand on his hip. "Levi is my partner in Bluegrass Security."

"Oh, sorry. I suppose that gimp keeps him from climbing ladders and such."

Breathing deeply to hold his temper, Mac evenly responded, "That gimp was earned protecting you and your family in Afghanistan. Damned near lost his leg and suffers extreme pain because of it. None of us came home without scars."

Twisting the end of his mustache, Evanston clicked his tongue against the roof of his mouth. "Well, no offense I hope." As an aside he mumbled, "Thank you for your service."

Nodding, Mac followed him into the barn, carrying two boxes of cameras and his laptop, Chuck following behind with a stack of boxes.

Hours later, sweaty, tired, and ready for a jump in the lake, Mac stood in the apron of the barn, laptop opened and resting on the ledge of an empty stall, testing each camera. He had his phone to his ear, Chuck on the other end in one of the pastures, as they tested their equipment. The sound of a vehicle pulling up next to his truck caused him to turn and stare. He muttered, "I'll be damned."

"What?"

Speaking into the phone, he replied, "Nothing. Call when you get to the east pasture."

Stevie jumped from her white Jeep, the halo around her head from the sun still present. She sauntered into the barn as if she'd been here before and stopped dead in her tracks as her eyes landed on his. Long moments later, she slowly turned her head and read the logo on the side of his truck.

5

"You work at Bluegrass Security?" She stopped a few feet from Mac; her heart beat out a wild tune in her chest. Seeing him again affected her more than she'd like. Dammit.

"I own Bluegrass Security." He said the word 'own' as if she should have known that.

She nodded and pulled her lips into a straight line. Their eyes locked on each other and she only hoped she was pulling off the casual pose she strived for because the butterflies flying around her stomach and her ragged breathing threatened to make her weak in the knees. His dark eyes and the dark smattering of hair peeking from the unbuttoned top of his white shirt made her cheeks warm. Remembering the crisp chest hairs as they brushed against her breasts just yesterday brought back the way she felt in his arms. If she allowed herself to close her eyes, she could still smell his aftershave.

One side of his lips lifted in a knowing smirk. The damn man knew he affected her and that rankled.

"Well, well, well. Detective Jorgenson, to what do I owe the pleasure of your company?"

The voice of Evanston Carlson grated on her nerves. The grotesque man she'd grown up with had spent the past forty years trying to outlive the past his father had sullied. Doping their horses to make them run beyond their physical abilities had won them a Derby, but that title was taken away as soon as it was discovered that they'd been doping their horses to the point of them running until they dropped dead. It was disgusting beyond words. On top of that, they'd poisoned some of the competition just before the race, and Carlson Sr. spent the rest of his life in jail.

"I'm here to ask you a few questions, Evie."

"That so?"

He moved his portly body so he stood close to Mac and across from her. Her eyes darted between the two men and irritation rose quickly. Mac was working for this asshole.

She pulled a notepad and pen from the back pocket of her jeans and opened the pad to the first clean page.

"That's so." She swung her gaze to Mac. "What are you doing here today?" She knew that came out kind of bitchy, but she couldn't help herself. She needed to get her detective face back on.

He cleared his throat, and his brows dipped just a bit before he answered. "Installing a security system. It's what we do at Bluegrass Security." He smiled at that point, and she tried to will the pink from her cheeks at asking such an amateur question.

She hesitated as his voice floated over her, and dammit, her nipples puckered. She wrote down his answer and the date and time, just to avoid looking at him. When she looked up from her notebook, she caught the smirk on his face and heard the chuckle he emitted and quickly glanced at Carlson.

"What do you need security for, Evie?" There that was better, her voice calmed.

"What does anyone need security for, Stevie? Evil lurks everywhere, and now that things are looking up here, it's time to secure my livestock. I've got a couple of Derby contenders here for next year, and I want to keep them safe."

She stared him in the eyes waiting for a twitch, proud that she didn't react when she saw one.

"Why do you think they wouldn't be safe?"

"No reason."

She took a deep breath and let it out slowly. She risked a glance at Mac, and he was still watching her. He stood a bit taller now, hands on his narrow hips and she couldn't stop herself following the lines his strong fingers made as they dipped into his front pockets and rested at the first knuckle.

"I need to know where you were last night, Evie."

She stared at her nemesis and hoped he'd give her some indication of his guilt or complicity in her father's mare being poisoned.

"I was here all night. You should feel free to go on up to the house and ask Caroline." He reached out with a pudgy hand and pointed to the house. "She hasn't seen you in a long time now. What's it been? Since the Derby last year?"

"Something like that." She made a few more notes in her book and waited for Mac to walk away, but he seemed amused by her presence.

Evanston took that moment to turn to Mac. "Mr. McKenzie, I get the feeling that Detective Jorgenson thinks I'm guilty of something, don't you?"

He chuckled, and she could see his crooked teeth which were still a sickly shade of yellow. He'd been teased mercilessly in school. The kids had called him Pissmouth. She'd never teased him; it seemed too damn mean, even though in her mind, she had reason to be mean to him. Their families had been bitter enemies since the drugging. Her father and grandfather before him couldn't stand it when animals were abused, and she'd grown up with a dislike of the Carlsons.

She eyeballed Mac and saw his brows dipped again before turning to his computer and tapping a few keys. "I'm not sure what she thinks. Probably be damned impossible to figure her out," he muttered.

Sting. "What is that supposed ..." She huffed and watched him turn his side to her. She felt dismissed, which made her stomach sour and her heart thud.

"Never mind." She walked toward her Jeep and Evie followed her. "Any of your horses come up sick in the last day or two?"

She watched his meaty hand twist his mustache, and her stomach turned again. "Not that I can say. Nope."

She looked around the ranch, at least what she could see. No search warrant meant she had no permission to investigate anything, and she honestly didn't know what she thought she'd find here. But she promised her father she'd help out, so she was interviewing the ranchers in the area. She'd come here last because she wanted to see if Evie's story was different than the others and it was. Another rancher had suffered a poisoned mare last night as well. And yet another had his barn broken into, but none of his horses were sick, and nothing had been stolen.

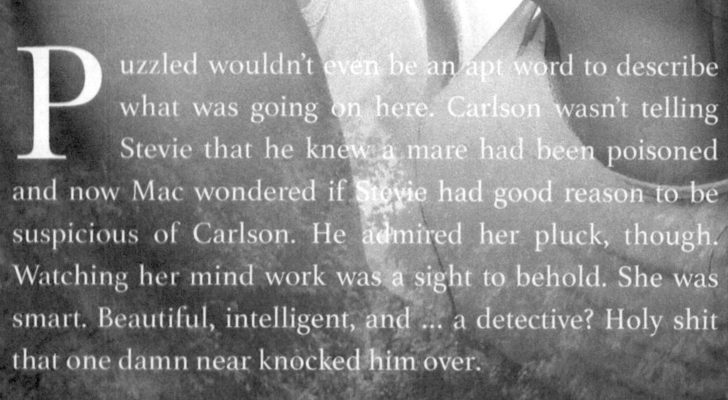

6

Puzzled wouldn't even be an apt word to describe what was going on here. Carlson wasn't telling Stevie that he knew a mare had been poisoned and now Mac wondered if Stevie had good reason to be suspicious of Carlson. He admired her pluck, though. Watching her mind work was a sight to behold. She was smart. Beautiful, intelligent, and ... a detective? Holy shit that one damn near knocked him over.

She acknowledged his presence but didn't give him any sign that she wanted to see him again. He'd already decided he couldn't get into any sort of relationship with her. She didn't seem like the relationship type for one, but, well he just couldn't go through getting his heart broken again. Still bugged him though.

He watched her intelligent eyes as she spoke with Carlson. Evie. It seemed she'd known him all her life, and she probably had. Bourbonville was a small town, and the folks around here seemed to stay forever. Ranch life wasn't something you just picked up and moved, and the finest racetracks and trainers were here. Once a rancher was established, he stayed. He watched as Stevie and Carlson stood next to her vehicle and continued their discussion. The jeans she wore hugged her toned body and the blue blouse she wore made her eyes sparkle. She stood with her back straight, but she was trying to look casual. She reached back and tucked the notebook into her back pocket, and his eyes were glued to the shape of her full breasts as her blouse stretched tight. Shit.

He finished adjusting the final camera in the far field with a few clicks on his computer. Closing the lid on his laptop, he fought the urge to look at Stevie. But, he lost. She happened to look at him at that same moment and the butterflies that flew through his stomach at that moment made him feel light-headed. Probably from being hot and tired all day.

"All done out back, Mac." Chuck ambled through the back barn door; his face was shiny from sweating. He stopped next to Mac but watched Stevie talking to Carlson.

"Hey, isn't that the woman—"

"Yes. Never mind."

Chuck snorted and began packing up the storage totes they'd brought their equipment in. All of the plastic bags and wire ties were picked up and tossed into one tote for garbage.

Mac finished writing the notes into his computer of all of the equipment used, the location of each of the cameras, and the necessary usernames and passwords Carlson would need to access them should he choose. Of course,

Sage and the crew would be monitoring things from the office and storing the recordings by day in the archive files.

He looked up to see Stevie writing in her notebook, and the ranch hand, George, he'd met this morning talking to her and Carlson. George seemed to be trying to make her laugh, and that pissed him off. At one point he leaned in and said something to Stevie, and he was so close to her he could have kissed her. That pissed him off even more. He took a step toward them and heard Chuck snicker. He froze and leveled a glare on him that made the big man blush. He quickly closed the lid on the tote he was packing and carried it toward Mac's truck.

Mac grabbed a couple of the totes, slung his laptop over his shoulder and tried looking casual as he stepped alongside Stevie and his truck. He wanted to make her sting like he did, so he pretended not to notice her as he walked by, but when she looked up at him, he couldn't resist. The bright blue of her eyes locked on his was like a blow to the stomach. He emitted a grunt and forced himself forward to the box of his truck.

Climbing into the driver's seat, he started his truck to get the air conditioning circulating. He checked his phone for messages and saw two from Sage, so he tapped a couple of icons and listened as she picked up.

"There you are. Finished at the Carlson ranch?"

"Yeah, Chuck's just putting the last of the totes in the back of the truck."

"Okay. We have another ranch job much like you did

today. Levi just came back, and the estimate is here for you. We told him you'd be out there tomorrow morning."

He glanced out his window as the cool air began blasting from the vents on the dash. The first blast that hit him brought with it the odor of his sweaty body, and he felt embarrassed about it for the first time in his life. He'd been sweaty enough in his life as he schlepped through battlefields in one desert or another. But, his mind wondered if Stevie had been able to smell him, and his eyes glanced at her noting that she looked perfectly cool and calm despite her tensed jaw. Then his eyes drifted to George, and he had the urge to jump from the truck and punch him in the face because his eyes were plastered to her breasts.

The truck dipped, and Chuck climbed in. The odor of sweat increased three-fold. Mac put the truck in reverse and slowly backed from his spot. A small smile hit his lips when Stevie turned and watched him drive away. Maybe she was interested.

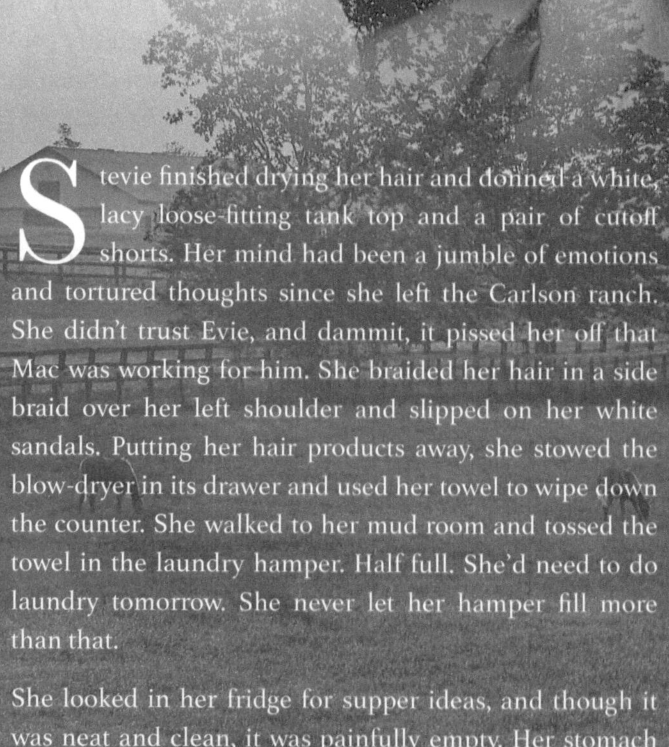

7

Stevie finished drying her hair and donned a white, lacy loose-fitting tank top and a pair of cutoff shorts. Her mind had been a jumble of emotions and tortured thoughts since she left the Carlson ranch. She didn't trust Evie, and dammit, it pissed her off that Mac was working for him. She braided her hair in a side braid over her left shoulder and slipped on her white sandals. Putting her hair products away, she stowed the blow-dryer in its drawer and used her towel to wipe down the counter. She walked to her mud room and tossed the towel in the laundry hamper. Half full. She'd need to do laundry tomorrow. She never let her hamper fill more than that.

She looked in her fridge for supper ideas, and though it was neat and clean, it was painfully empty. Her stomach turned as the image of Mac's face flitted through her mind. The expression he wore as he backed out of Carlson's parking apron was almost pained, though she didn't know him well enough to know for sure.

She turned to look around her kitchen. Her perfectly clean table held nothing but a small basket of flowers she'd won at last year's Bourbonville Park Carnival. Her mother had won it, but it didn't meet her mother's standards, and she quickly handed it off to her. Stevie, being practical and enjoying the fuchsia and purples in the basket, brought it home with her and that's where it had been since.

The fruit basket on the counter held only an apple. But the thought of eating right now twisted her stomach. Something wasn't right at the Carlson ranch, and it bugged her. Deciding she'd first see Mac and see if she could get him to tell her why he was truly at the Carlson ranch, then her tummy would quit flopping around, and she'd be able to eat. She'd grab some food and a game of pool or two at the Brass Rail. Ethan had the best fried chicken in the county, and he was easy on the eyes.

As she made her way downstairs, she mused at her detective status at the sheriff's office as it gave her access to many interesting records, including the county citizen's names and addresses. Came in handy sometimes—like today.

~

The scene up Mac's driveway was simply breathtaking. She remembered parking here as a teenager. At the time, Widow Majors lived here, and she always went to bed early. Stevie's boyfriend was Ethan Hastings' brother, Max. He also owned the Brass Rail with Ethan, but he was more the business partner of the team. Ethan was much more personable. But, at the time, she thought she was in love, then she realized Max loved Max and no one else, and she reluctantly broke off their relationship, not wanting to be a 'friend with benefits.' She went off to college after graduation, fell in love with Derek Groskopf, and had her heart soundly broken after three long years.

She frowned as she drove past the former 'parking spot' which was simply a little lane off the driveway.

As the white house came into view, a beautiful black and tan Belgian bounded from the house. It jumped and barked giving her the impression that he'd be a stellar watchdog but he was still puppyish and would no doubt happily welcome a scratch behind the ears and a treat. She pulled to a stop, reached into her glove box and pulled a dog treat from the bag she kept there. Living in a county like Chandler, she often found herself visiting ranches and farms where dogs lived and always wanted to make friends with them first. Tasty snacks made her popular.

She slowly opened her door and watched the pup's reaction. He continued to bark but made no move to advance on her, so she stepped from her Jeep, slowly extended her arm, and held the treat in front of her. The furry bundle froze, raised his nose into the air and sniffed. His tail wagged, and he slowly approached the proffered morsel. He gently sniffed again, then accepted the treat. Apparently, that was enough for him as he began licking her hand and sniffing her sandals, laying a wet swath across the top of her foot before bounding off toward the lake.

The water called to her, and she followed the dog toward the lake's edge. It was breathtaking with the sun glinting on the ripples. Ducks in the distance quacked their disapproval as the dog jumped into the water sending water flying in all directions. She laughed as the angry birds flew away giving him a piece of their mind. He dove under the water and came up a few feet away, jumped to shore and happily ran to her, stopping only to grab a bright green ball alongside a shrub.

She worried slightly that he wouldn't stop before he reached her, his speed as fast as a young thoroughbred. Dust kicked up as he stopped abruptly, his wet sloppy ball landing on the top of her foot. He promptly sat and patiently waited for her to toss it for him, so she obliged. Her years of softball came in handy as she tossed the ball into the lake, the happy mop of wet fur scurrying after it.

She laughed and clapped her hands together as their game continued a few more times. In the distance, she heard a vehicle approaching. The butterflies came to life in her belly, and she let out a long slow breath. She focused on the sun glinting on the water, the dog, birds flying overhead, anything to keep from thinking about seeing him again, which was stupid, it was why she was here, but suddenly it didn't seem like a great idea.

Mac's attention landed on the white Jeep in his driveway. "What the hell?" he mumbled.

He turned the radio off and rolled his window down; the sound of her laughter and Ammo's barking tightened his chest. He pulled to a stop next to her vehicle and slowly stepped out, stretched slightly and wandered toward her laughter.

She stood at the edge of the lake, her sexy tanned legs spattered with water, likely from Ammo. But what a sight. Short denim cutoffs were his kryptonite. The loose tank of white lace and gauzy material allowed the view of her silhouette when she raised her arm to toss the ball into the lake. He'd been instantly attracted to her the moment he saw her last night, but this—seeing her standing in his yard, playing with his dog, the sweet look of happiness on her face—made his heart thud.

He shook his head of the ridiculous thoughts and stepped toward her. "Do you always stop at people's homes and play with their dogs?"

She glanced back at him briefly before bending to pick up the ball and toss it again. "Don't make a habit of it, but your pup wanted to play, and I haven't tossed a ball in years."

The splash made her giggle, but she turned to face him. "Nice doggy door you have for him. Bet he loves being able to come outside when the mood strikes him."

Mac searched her face for signs of emotion, but being the detective she was, her expression was closed. "He does. Sometimes I have to work late and can't get here at reasonable times to let him out, so that was the perfect solution."

A gentle breeze blew a hint of her perfume over him, and he instantly remembered that he'd been sweating all day and took a step back. "Did you need something, detective?"

She placed her hands on her hips but didn't say anything for a long while. He tried not to glance at her breasts, but the tank allowed cleavage to show and he was a man after all.

Her brows bunched together before she asked, "Will you tell me why you were putting a security system in for Evie?"

She licked her lips, and all the blood in his body ran south. He stepped back and turned toward the back door. "Obviously, to secure his ranch. For a detective, that should have been a given."

He unlocked the door, twisted the handle, and remembering he had fried chicken in the truck, walked back to get it. He strode back to the house, and not wanting to be rude, he glanced back at her. "I need a shower. You're welcome to come in and wait till I get out. Then you can ask me more of your easy questions. Beer in the fridge; bourbon in the cupboard."

He waited and watched the indecision on her face. She glanced at Ammo trying to chase a butterfly, and the soft smile that played on her lips made his cock jump. She began walking toward him, and he stepped into the house. Tossing his keys and the container of chicken on the counter, he began pulling his sweaty shirt off as he walked down the hallway to his bathroom. He heard her enter the house and sigh before he rounded the corner. Unable to stop himself from looking back at her, he caught her eyes with his and was pleased that she seemed to enjoy the view. Good, because he'd enjoyed his too.

~

S tevie's stomach growled as the aroma of Ethan's fried chicken wafted to her nose. She turned from the hall where Mac had just rounded the corner, his sexy backside a thing of beauty, and walked to the kitchen cabinets to find the bourbon.

The water in the bathroom turned on, and she closed her eyes at the image that floated her way of a completely wet Mac rubbing soap on his extremely toned, sexy body. Wow. She found a bottle of Ethan's bourbon in a cabinet next to the refrigerator. She set it next to the chicken and began opening and closing the cabinet doors until she found the glasses. Pulling two plain highball glasses down, she poured them each one-third full, capped the bottle, and stared into the beautiful amber liquid. Her stomach growled again, and she heard the shower shut off.

Taking a deep breath to calm the new flutter in her stomach, she quickly turned to pull plates from the cupboard, forks from a drawer and napkins from the holder next to the stove. She glanced at the kitchen table but felt a bit bold. After all, she'd just invited herself to dinner, but it smelled so damned good, and she was suddenly starving. And, she loved Ethan's chicken. She just wanted to sit and talk to Mac. Just talk. Nothing more. Maybe get some pieces of the puzzle put in place.

The bathroom door opened and the man himself sauntered down the hall. A white T-shirt stretched across his broad chest, tan khaki shorts covered his thighs, but his lower legs and feet were bare. What the hell was it about a man's bare feet that had her damned near drooling? His eyes met hers and held. He stopped on the opposite side of the center island and the corner of his mouth lifted. "You're staying for dinner I see."

Pink tinted her cheeks, and her heart thundered in her chest. Her mouth opened, closed, then opened again. "I love Ethan's chicken, and I was going to stop in there tonight anyway. Kismet."

His brows rose into the dark, damp curls that fell onto his forehead. "Kismet?"

"You know—destiny, fate. We both thought about Ethan's chicken, and voila, here it is."

He shook his head but grabbed the container of food, set it on top of the plates and carried them to the table. "You grab the silverware and the booze."

He sat down, and she blinked as she realized how he dwarfed the table. His long legs bent and tucked under the wooden structure, and she had to stifle a giggle because he looked so out of place.

He glanced at her, his brows furrowed. "Sit."

She promptly set the silverware on the table and turned to pull their glasses from the counter. Setting them down she took the chair directly across from him. The scent of the man fresh from the shower and the chicken would all but undo her, and she needed to keep her head straight.

"So why were you really at Evie's today?"

He bit into a leg; the crisp breading crunched loudly. She pulled a piece of white meat from the container and bit into it, stifling the moan as her mouth was so grateful for the taste.

He swallowed, picked up his bourbon and drank down a hefty mouthful. "I thought I already answered that, detective. I installed a security system. Anything else is business and not for sharing." He bit into the leg again, the rest of the meat falling off the bone and into his kissable mouth. He licked a crumb from his bottom lip, and she tightened her knees together against the pulsing that rushed to her lower regions. "Unless of course, you have a warrant to see any of my records. Which you don't, or you'd have shown it to me first."

She shrugged, bit into her chicken again and closed her eyes. Best. Chicken. Ever. "I'm just curious. He has a colorful past, and he doesn't have the kind of money to go and have an expensive security system installed. I checked, you guys aren't cheap."

He opened his mouth to say something, and she quickly held up a couple of fingers. "I didn't say you weren't worth it, just that you cost a few bucks. Evie doesn't have it."

"How do you know? You have access to his bank records?"

She picked up another piece of chicken and bit into it. "Of course not. I've known him almost my whole life. His daddy almost lost the ranch years ago. Ruined their reputation and he's struggled to change things since. But he's impetuous, and in his zeal to turn the ranch around, he's made some major mistakes."

Mac's lips pursed slightly before he responded. "Like what kind of mistakes?"

She searched his eyes for sincerity, the dark shiny orbs mesmerizing. Setting her half-finished piece of chicken on her plate, she wiped her fingers on the napkin alongside and said, "Ten years ago, he almost lost the ranch. Things were bad, and he'd begun to sell off some of the equipment. The banks wouldn't touch him, and realtors were swarming hoping to grab the listing. Caroline, his wife, begged her daddy for some money to help them with stud fees to breed a mare that had promise."

She took a drink of her bourbon and paused as the warmth flowed all the way down her throat. "Her daddy agreed after an enormous amount of begging and Evie being Evie, took it to the Red Mile Casino in Lexington. Thought he could double it or triple it. He ended up meeting a bookie who talked him into a horse race circuit, and Evie bet it all and more. He lost it. Of course. Ended up owing the bookie two thousand dollars to boot."

Picking up the remainder of her chicken, she bit into the juicy morsel and stifled the moan she wanted to unleash.

Mac set the bones on his plate and leaned forward, forearms on the table. "Well? What happened?"

She licked her lips and smiled broadly. "He sold his prize mare to pay back his father-in-law and the bookie."

He held her eyes for a while, and she could see his wheels turning. He picked up another piece of chicken, and just before biting into it, he replied, "That was ten years ago. A lot can happen in ten years."

"Not for Evie. Unless he's into something illegal."

8

Eating dinner with Stevie was nice. She kept the conversation flowing, and it wasn't uncomfortable. Even when they weren't talking it was casual and light. Sitting across from her gave him the added bonus of looking at her. She was a feast for his eyes. Without hesitation, she dug in and picked up a piece of chicken without looking for a fork. She ate with gusto where most women would look around for a salad and eat a leaf. Not Stevie.

Finishing the last piece of chicken, he leaned back in his chair and picked up his bourbon. The amber liquid caught the light streaming in from the window as he swished his glass and the swirls caught his attention. Lifting the glass to his lips, his eyes landed on Stevie as she swallowed the remaining spirits in her glass. Her eyes slid shut as she swallowed, and he froze as the serene look on her face appeared.

Slowly the baby blues opened and pinned him where he sat. "I love Ethan's new blend. Actually all of his blends, but this one, has a hint of the smoky oak barrel he used, and it's simply perfect."

He swallowed down the remainder of his liquid and reached for the bottle pouring each of them another. "You seem to know a lot about Ethan's distilling methods."

She shrugged. "Yeah, I guess. He likes telling me about it, and I like listening."

Ouch. That sharp pain that hit his heart hurt. But that was simply stupid because ... well, it was stupid. "Have you dated him?"

She laughed and the sound was musical. "No. I used to date his brother, Max, in high school, but Ethan and I have always been good friends. And it's nice talking to someone about anything that isn't illegal or work related."

Ouch. Well, that just hurt too. Her work, or at least her suspicions, had been the primary topic of conversation during dinner. Here he'd thought they were having a great conversation and she was bored. He cleared his throat and stood to clear their dirty dishes. He emptied the chicken bones in the container from the Brass Rail, then wrapped the box in a plastic bag, tying it closed at the top. "I'll be right back."

He tossed the offensive bones into the garbage bin just outside his garage door. When he walked into the kitchen, Stevie wasn't there. His brows furrowed and he turned the corner to the living room. There she stood in front of his entertainment center, looking at his pictures. He stood alongside her and followed her line of sight. The picture was taken on base in Afghanistan; they were in uniform and had just come back from a particularly dreadful mission. They were sweaty and dirty, and the smiles on their faces seemed especially bright since the dirt caked on their faces made them look so dark. "That's Levi, my partner. One of them." He pointed.

"I recognized him." She looked at another and touched the picture of Levi lying in a hospital bed, bandages covering most of him after he'd been hit with the IED.

"That was two days after we'd been hit." She swallowed and slowly turned to look into his eyes.

"We?"

Not wanting to be morose, he sucked in a breath and let it out slowly. "We were on patrol, our whole unit. Levi and I were walking behind the Humvee with three of our brothers. The Humvee tripped an IED and Levi being just in front and to the right of me caught more shrapnel than I did. He was ripped up pretty good. Still bears nasty scars and suffers pain every day. Damn near lost his leg."

"Oh," she said softly as she stared into his eyes. Hers glistened with unshed tears, and he couldn't help it, so he touched her face softly with this fingers. Her scent wrapped around him, the aroma of spring fresh laundry soap and peaches, and the heat rolling off of her claimed him. He leaned in and slowly touched his lips to hers. Once. Twice. Then his tongue decided for itself to go in and play. She tasted of supper and bourbon, and the exquisite feel of her velvety tongue sliding along his damned near undid him. She grabbed his shirt with both hands at the sides, and he imagined she was hanging on for the ride. At least he hoped. He wrapped his arms around her and pulled her to him, her ample breasts smashed against his chest and her soft belly made for the perfect cushion for his quickly growing cock.

He heard her whimper, and his heartbeat sped up.

He slid a hand over her ass and pushed her farther into him, and she groaned. At least he thought so, but he groaned too and it drowned her out. He commanded her mouth, then kissed his way down her throat. He nipped the soft skin just under her ear, and he heard her whisper, "Yes," so softly he wasn't completely sure, but he felt like saying that himself, so, he was pretty sure she said it.

She tugged at his T-shirt, pulling it from his shorts, her warm hands flattened on his sides and slid up his back. She moved them around, part massaging him—part exciting the fuck out of him.

Ammo came bounding in at that moment and dropped an empty dish on his foot. The tin bowl sounded like a bad drum, and it raced back to his mind that in the excitement of Stevie being here, he'd forgotten to feed his poor pup.

He leaned his forehead on Stevie's for just a moment, holding her sweet face between his hands, willing his breathing to slow. When he could say something, he chuckled. "I forgot to feed the baby. Hang on, and I'll be right back."

He kissed her lips lightly then leaned to pick up Ammo's bowl. "Come on, boy, let's get you fed, and I'm sorry." He patted his pup on the head and walked to the kitchen, the excited mass of damp fur jumping behind and around him.

She froze as she watched him pat his dog on the head. Baby. There it was again. What the hell was wrong with her; she couldn't get involved with him. Clearly, he was into the whole settling down, get a dog, and have a baby thing. She softly swiped the worry from her face with her fingers and blew out a soft breath. She plastered on a soft smile and followed Mac into the kitchen. She watched him fill Ammo's dish with food, then with a simple hand signal, asked him to sit and wait. Once Ammo's butt hit the floor, he set the dish down into its wrought iron holder and picked up the matching water dish. He walked to the sink, dumped the old water in the dish, and rinsed the bowl. He filled it with cool water and set it alongside the food dish in the holder. He stood, his eyes on Ammo. He walked to the cupboard, pulled a plastic cup down and pushed it against the ice dispenser in his refrigerator door. His eyes were on his pup as he slowly poured the ice into the dish of water. Once he stepped back, he said, "Okay."

Ammo attacked his food with vigor. Mac chuckled then turned to her. "Sorry, I try to keep him on a schedule, and I completely forgot. I guess I'm a bad fur parent."

The air whooshed from her lungs, and her stupid eyes moistened. She swallowed and stepped to the back door where she'd come in. "No worries, a guy's gotta eat. I've got to get rolling. You have a good night."

Before he could say a word to her, she flew through the door and walked as quickly as she could to her Jeep. She jumped in and backed from the driveway as a tear slipped from her eye. Must be allergies.

9

M ac loosened his grip on the steering wheel. He'd been squeezing it so tight his hand ached. Didn't help that his head pounded so much that it could rival the drums in Steppenwolf's *Born to be Wild*. He stretched his shoulders back and slowly let out a breath.

"I can drive if you need to relax, Mac," Dirks, one of his partners and very good friend, said as he scrutinized him from the passenger seat.

"I'm okay."

"Didn't ask if you were okay. I simply said I could drive. You've been out of sorts all day. Ready to talk about it yet?"

"No."

The side - glance Dirks gave him mirrored his thoughts. *Yeah, right.*

Dirks leaned forward and pulled a bottle of water from the cooler on the floor between his feet. Twisting the plastic top, he handed it to Mac. Taking the cold bottle in his hand Mac sipped at the water, enjoying the cool slide down his throat. Dirks leaned forward and grabbed another water and opened it. He guzzled down half the bottle, then leaned his head against the rest.

He glanced over at his friend and felt bad about what a jerk he'd been all day. They'd worked on a security system in Bloomin' Petals, a little flower shop here in Bourbonville, and he'd barely said ten words to Dirks. When he did say something, he snapped out his answer. It didn't take his friend long to decide to leave well enough alone. Thanks to him, they'd had a silent, tense day when it could have been pleasant. There was no reason to be an ass to Dirks.

"I think I met someone," he huffed out.

Dirks turned his head, a big grin on his face. "How do you 'think' you've met someone? You either have, or you haven't."

Shrugging, he sipped at his water, eyes on the road ahead. They were heading out to the Carlson ranch to check on the new system. It was something they did as a courtesy since after a day or two the clients usually had questions.

"I mean, I met someone, but she doesn't like me."

Dirks turned his head and stared at him for a long time. Too long. Then he laughed a full belly laugh. "I doubt that's true." He drank down a healthy portion of his water and glanced out the window. "Women always like you. What's not to like? Tall, dark, and handsome. Not like me, short, blond, and average."

Now it was Mac's turn to laugh. "As I recall it, when we were on leave in California, you were with a bevy of gals over the long weekend. I was the one standing on the sidelines watching."

"Yeah, but you'd just dumped Brenda, and you were pissy and moody. Girls can spot moody a mile away."

Mac scowled at the mention of Brenda's name. He'd dated her for a little more than two years which, while enlisted, is a feat. They'd managed to stay together during one base move, and things seemed as though they were good. Then he'd found a note in her rucksack from a fellow soldier. It turns out, she'd been seeing him for almost the same amount of time.

"Yeah." Thoughts of Stevie flew through his mind. She'd picked him up in no time and walked him across the back yard and to her apartment where she'd stripped and had sex with him in a matter of a few minutes. Simple as that. He reminded himself she probably did that often, and he sure didn't need to go through that heartache again.

He turned down the long drive to the Carlson ranch. Activity was nil today to the point of almost creepy. Dirks must have felt it too as he sat forward in his seat and peered out the windshield. No horses were grazing in the pastures, and no one appeared to be walking around or working the fields. A quick glance at the house noted a newer Audi A8. Pricey. Stevie had said Carlson didn't have money, so that couldn't be his car. An older Ford pickup sat against a shed just behind the house. Mac turned left toward the barn. As he put the truck in park, he looked around for any signs of life. Nothing. Glancing at Dirks, he shrugged as Dirks' brows rose. "Might as well go see what's up."

The oppressive heat enveloped him as he exited the truck; he had a fleeting thought to jump back in and go home. He and Dirks slowly made their way toward the entrance when a door slammed at the house. Mac turned to see a well-dressed Hispanic-looking man walking toward the Audi. He had mocha-colored skin, dressed in a tan business suit with a light sheen on it. When the man looked his way, his dark eyes looked right through him, and the warning crawl of dread filled Mac's stomach. The man simply nodded once and smoothly seated himself in the Audi. The engine roared to life, the purring of the expensive engine something to admire. He slowly backed from his parking spot, shifted into gear, and purred down the long drive.

Once he was out of sight, Mac looked toward the house to see Carlson standing on the covered front porch glaring at him. "Hello there." His jovial greeting didn't match the glower in his hazel eyes.

"Hello, Mr. Carlson. I'd like to introduce you to Dirks, one of my partners."

Carlson walked toward them, glancing briefly down the drive after the Audi. The furrow in his brows was interesting. As he neared them, he plastered on a smile and held his hand out to Dirks as he greeted him.

After shaking hands, Carlson slid his hands into his pants pockets. Dirks started explaining their purpose for being here, and Mac tuned out as he tried to covertly glance around at the inactivity on the ranch. They were just two weeks from the Derby and even the ranches that didn't have a horse in the race had an enormous amount of activity at their ranches. Just day-to-day tasks required people to be working.

The men entered the barn to check the office computer and answer a couple of the questions Carlson had. All of the stalls were occupied which explained why there weren't any horses outside grazing. Large fans circulated the air attempting to cool the livestock inside. One stall just across from the office held bags of grain with the company name of RRI on it. When he and Chuck had installed the security system, he'd been in the grain barn, so why was there a specific grain in here? A ranch hand entered the barn from the back and nodded to Mac before closing the stall door holding the grain.

As Dirks finished answering Carlson's questions, they were quickly ushered out of the barn. Shaking hands with Carlson, the two men climbed into the truck, and as he started the engine to start the air cooling down the inside, he looked at Dirks. "Grab your tablet and pull up this ranch." Mac pulled his phone out and held it to his ear so it looked like he was talking.

The puzzled look on Dirks' face didn't stop him from doing what he was told. As he logged into the Whispering Cave's system, Mac said, "Pull up the barn office and see if you can zero in on the grain in the stall across from the office."

10

Stevie sat at her desk in the Sheriff's Department finishing up paperwork. The poisoning of area horses—and yes there had been another poisoning this morning at the Open Caves Ranch owned by the Browns—was beginning to look like a serial poisoner was on the loose. Her father's mare was still lingering, though it was unlikely she'd ever be able to race. Her heart was damaged beyond repair. The horse from this morning, however, had passed.

Looked like another busy day ahead of her, and the heat was oppressive today. At just nine o'clock in the morning, it was already eighty-eight degrees and climbing, and she would be out investigating and interviewing the ranch hands at Open Caves. Saving this morning's report, she prepared to leave the office when her phone rang. "Detective Jorgenson."

"Detective, this is Archer Davids. I need you to come out to the ranch; I've had a horse poisoned."

His weary voice clenched her stomach. It was the voice of her father and the other rancher who'd had horses go down last night. "I'll be right out, Mr. Davids."

She took the important information she needed, location, timing, etc. and quickly made her way through the office, grabbing a bottle of water from the cooler. Climbing into her Jeep, she spied a tan dog, and its owner walking across the little park and her thoughts flew to Mac. Her mind wandered to his handsome face and the way he smelled. He always smelled so good, fresh, and clean. When he touched her, it was like her heart sang. Which seemed stupid; she barely knew him. She shook her head and started her vehicle. She needed to get him out of her head. He wanted a family, and she couldn't offer him that. He needed to be with someone who could. He deserved that, didn't he? Well, she'd just stay away from him, and they could both just move on. How hard could it be? He'd been here for three months or so, and she'd managed to not meet him until this past week. Working with her family at Balmoral would help her avoid seeing him. If she watched for his pickup truck outside of the Brass Rail, she'd be able to squeeze in a game of pool or so before turning in for the night. Of course, Bluegrass Security was just across Main Street from the Brass Rail, so she'd have to watch that he wasn't at the office first. Why did life have to be so damned complicated?

Leaning forward, she twisted the knob on the dash to increase the cool air blowing into her vehicle. Damned humidity would suffocate her before the day was through. The Davids' ranch was just outside of Bourbonville on the way to Chandlerville and just before Fire Lake. In other words, a short distance. When she pulled into the drive, she saw a large truck with the lettering, *Kentucky Animal Pickup and Rendering* on the side. Not good. That meant the horse didn't make it and they'd called the disposal company to take it away. In this heat, they'd remove it as soon as they could. Doc Burgis was there as well with her white medical van with many doors on the outside carrying most everything she needed as time was usually of the essence. Many of the ranch hands milled about chatting with each other as well. She brusquely walked into the activity and introduced herself to those who didn't know her.

"Detective, this has got to stop. This is the third poisoning this week, and all of us with contenders are feeling targeted." Archer's middle-aged face shined with sweat. The firm set of his jaw and the jerkiness of his movements told of his distress.

"I promise you we're working on it, Mr. Davids. Let's go over some specifics."

She maintained her professional demeanor as she interviewed each of the hands and Davids. When she felt she had all of the questions answered, she approached Deanne Burgis. "Doc, did the lab results come back from my dad's horse?"

Deanne was a slight woman of only five feet tall, slender build, and long copper hair pulled into a ponytail at her nape. She never wore makeup; she didn't need it. Her natural beauty was enough to take your breath away. The crisp green eyes amid the darkness of her hair and brows were so mesmerizing it was often hard to look away from her. In her mid- to late-thirties Doc was younger than her by around five years or so.

"I'm afraid I just got them this morning. It looks like Nerium Oleander was ingested. I haven't told your father yet."

Stevie was speechless. Any horse rancher worth a salt scoured their fields regularly to ensure the offensive Oleander wasn't growing anywhere close to where a horse could eat it. She knew her father sprayed regularly.

"Do you think it's the same thing with this horse? This morning I was out at the Open Caves Ranch where another poisoning had occurred."

"I was called to the renderer's to take a sample on that horse, and it's been sent to the lab. I've asked for a rush since we seem to be in the midst of something nefarious here."

Smiling at the doc she said, "Thanks, Doc. Definitely something that is more than a coincidence. There are at least ten miles separating Balmoral, from Open Caves to here. The Oleander isn't blowing in the wind and depositing itself here. What's your take on it?"

The petite woman fanned herself with the notebook she carried. "I called the Ag specialist over at the university this morning and chatted with him. He was on his way to Balmoral after we spoke. When I heard of the incident at Open Caves, I called him back and told him about it. I'll be calling him in the truck to ask him also to inspect the crops here." She turned her head as a vehicle pulled in behind the Jeep. Bluegrass Security was written across the side of the truck, and Stevie held her breath. Mac stepped from the vehicle, his jeans fitting him perfectly, the light blue, button-up shirt he wore giving off the impression he was cool and collected. When he pierced her with his eyes, moisture gathered between her legs and her stomach flipped. A shiver raced down her spine, and she silently cursed under her breath. "Shit."

Doc Burgis observed her silently, and a small smile appeared on her lips when she glanced in Mac's direction. That ugly little monster inside of Stevie reared up so fast it almost made her dizzy at the thought that Doc Burgis would show interest. Then her stomach clenched tighter, if that were possible, when Doc said, "Well, my goodness, look at that tall drink of water. New blood and mmm, mmm, mighty fine."

Stevie's jaw tightened, but she couldn't stop herself. She watched the man of their attentions saunter toward them, his swagger a thing of beauty. Sexy. Sure. Amazing. The heat in her cheeks had nothing to do with the weather. To her amazement, he didn't look at Doc, but his eyes locked on hers, and as he neared the fresh scent of his shower soap and aftershave wafted toward her, and dammit, her nipples puckered.

"Detective." His deep voice floated over her, and her heartbeat sped up.

"Sam," she managed, but it came out strained.

"Hello, I'm Deanne Burgis, the area veterinarian." The small woman looked dwarfed next to Mac's six-foot two-ish frame. And when he reached his hand out to shake Doc's, she had to swallow the bitterness that flooded into her mouth.

"Sam McKenzie of Bluegrass Security. Pleasure to meet you."

Did she just hear Doc giggle? Oh my gawd, she did. The look of pure awe on the good doctor's face infuriated her to no end. "You're quite popular these days. If I didn't know better, I'd say these poisonings are a boon to Bluegrass Security."

Oops, the look he pinned her with seemed deadly. Scary. When he spoke, his voice was low and his words deliberate. "Detective, I know you don't know me all that well. You'd get to know me better if you didn't run off, by the way." He leaned into her space, and she swallowed. "But I would never do anything to hurt an animal just for financial gain. My partners are the same."

The tightness in his jaw was unmistakable, and she felt instantly sorry she'd said anything. Lashing out for something that had nothing to do with anything other than she was jealous. Well, that was petty. And, didn't she just tell herself that he should move on? She did. Why did that hurt so damn much?

"Well, it appears there's more going on here than I'm aware, so I'll take my leave and get these samples to the lab." Doc reached into the pocket of her white lab coat and pulled out a business card. Handing it to Mac, she smiled sweetly. "If I can be of assistance in any way, Mr. McKenzie, please feel free to give me a call."

He smiled at Doc. HE SMILED AT DOC! That was it. Enough. He nodded and then and she climbed into her van with a glance back at him. He wasn't looking at the doctor, though; he was looking at her. As the van pulled away, his deep raspy voice broke into her dark cloud of anger. "You owe me an apology."

She sucked in a breath, swallowed, and dared a look into the dark eyes she found so mesmerizing. Softly she said, "Sorry."

"Not good enough."

"What?"

"Not good enough."

She squared her body to his. "I'm very sorry!" she huffed out.

"Nope."

"What do you mean 'nope'?"

"Need to do better."

She was becoming exasperated. "Tell me what type of apology you're looking for?"

"Hmm. I'll think of something."

She stared. No words came to her. She was hot, sweat dripping down her face, her armpits were damp, and damn it all, he looked like he just stepped from the shower. Smelled damn good too.

The grin on his face dented one of his dimples into his cheek, and she tried not to look at it. She really did. Tried hard.

He walked away, seemingly proud of himself as Archer waved him over. She watched him as he chatted away. Though he glanced her way often, her emotions were a jumble. She was supposed to be avoiding him. The damned fates kept throwing them together. This was wrong on so many levels because she was going to get tangled up with Mac and then her heart was going to be trampled, stomped, and kicked to the curb. She rubbed her temples as the headache started adding pressure.

"Detective?" She turned to see a ranch hand standing before her. "I found this." He held up a white flower on a short branch that looked of an evergreen variety. Oleander.

"Where did you find this?"

He turned and pointed to a pasture past the barn. "Over that hill there is our east pasture, and it was along the fence line, just under it." He pointed to the horse being loaded into the rendering truck. "He was in that pasture yesterday."

11

Mac finished chatting with Archer Davids, wrote up a brief estimate, and headed back to the office. One thing Stevie was right about; these horse poisonings were a boon to Bluegrass Security, and on the one hand, he was grateful. But on the other hand, he hated seeing these ranchers so devastated. This was their very livelihood, and he hated what was happening to them. Remembering his own family farm and his father's struggles made his stomach clench. He and Levi had grown up two hours from Bourbonville in a little town in the southern part of the state. Dirt poor, both of them, it's what pushed them both to enlist and get out of there.

He entered the office where thankfully the air was cool and the office fairly quiet. The only person in right now was Levi. He was a master at writing up their estimates. Plus, with his bum leg, it kept him from having to walk around an inordinate amount.

Pulling the paperwork from his briefcase, he set it on Levi's desk. "From the Davids' ranch this morning. I told him we'd try and get out there tomorrow."

Levi picked up the papers and looked them over quickly. "Doable. Our new stock came in this morning, so we should have enough. At this rate, I'll be ordering daily."

Sam sat behind Sage's desk and leaned back, plopping his feet on the top. Levi glanced over at him. "You still want me to investigate the good detective?"

"Yep."

Levi stood and stretched, grabbed his coffee cup from the top of the desk and went to the pot to refill it. Turning around, Levi leveled his eyes on him. "If she finds out, she's going to be pissed off."

Shrugging his shoulders slightly, he responded. "Then she can't find out. I need to know what kind of person she is Levi. I can't go through the betrayal again. You know exactly what I mean by that."

Levi stopped and stared at him. He'd been betrayed in the same way; only it probably hurt a bit more. He'd been engaged and planning a wedding when his fiancée, Jenny, sent him a Dear John letter that she was marrying a good friend of theirs from high school, Tim.

"Be discreet."

Sitting with a thud, Levi began tapping away on the keyboard to finish his work. "I'm always discreet."

He'd asked Levi to do a bit of research on Stevie. Since he couldn't get her out of his head, he decided to figure out what she was all about. Levi and Sage could ferret out information like no one he knew.

He leaned forward. "Where's Dirks?"

"Surveillance. The new client who came in yesterday who thinks her husband is cheating on her? Dirks is watching him. Might need you to relieve him later on."

"Sounds good. I'll check in with him."

He and Dirks were the muscle and Levi and Sage were their geeks. Of course, Chuck was muscle too, but the big ole' farm boy didn't have the training and experience twenty-five years in the Army had given him and Dirks, so Chuck was more or less relegated to installations only- for now.

Levi's phone rang, and he grabbed it before the second ring, punching the icon to answer the call. "Bluegrass Security."

Leaning back in his chair, Levi slid a glance toward him, a grin on his face. "Yes, sir, Mr. Jorgenson. I'll send Mac out right away to talk with you about our offerings."

He ended the call and grinned a bit wider. "Looks like your girl's daddy has decided on a new security system. So, you're gonna go and make nice with him. Just give me the basics like you did with this one, and I'll pull something together. Things keep going like this, and we're going to need to hire someone else so we can keep an eye on all of these systems. I'm going to have Sage write up an ad, and we'll start interviewing as soon as we have some great candidates."

Running his hands through his hair, he stemmed the roiling in his stomach as he prepared himself to meet Stevie's father. He glanced out the window to the street and stared at the front of The Brass Rail. He'd only been in the bar twice, and the second time he'd met Stevie. Her face filled his head. Clear skin and those crisp blue eyes damn near wound him right around her little finger. Her tits were a thing of beauty—full, round, and firm. He could still remember how they felt in his hands. Her smooth, heated skin, her tits pliable, and her nipples pointed and firm. He closed his eyes and remembered her perfume and the little moans she made as he pushed himself into her had lulled him to sleep each night since. Every time he saw her, heard her voice, he remembered how they sounded together.

He opened his eyes and slightly shook his head. He needed to get over this. The car that had pulled up to the curb across the street caught his attention.

"Levi, see what you can find out on that car over there, will you?"

Levi stood with a groan and limped to the window. "The Audi?" He pulled his phone from his back pocket and took a picture of the car and the plates. "What's up with that?"

Mac explained that he'd seen that car and the man getting out of it at the Carlson farm and that things had seemed weird.

"Hmm. Okay," his friend mused as he turned back to his desk and began tapping on his keyboard.

The man unfolded himself from the car and opened the back door. He was thin, not especially tall, and his extremely dark hair had a bit of a curl to it, though it was cut fairly short. The sun reflected from it and cast highlights in the curls. He wore expensive looking dress slacks in a soft gray color and a crisp white button-up dress shirt. His tie was a deep gray, and as he reached into the car, the thick gold watchband caught his attention. He pulled a soft gray sports coat from the back seat and slipped it on as he walked toward The Brass Rail. Lunch hour. Perfect timing. Sucking down the last of his water, Mac tossed the empty bottle in the recycle bin as he said over his shoulder, "I'm going to see if I can engage him in conversation. While I'm there, you want something to eat?"

Levi nodded. "Sage is there right now getting us some of Ethan's fried chicken. I've heard it's the best around."

Mac's steps faltered remembering Stevie's lips as she licked the chicken juices and crumbs from them. A twitch in his pants had him pulling the door open harder than he needed. He shook the memories from his mind and strutted across the street, watching for traffic as he navigated to the bar. He really needed to figure out what it was about Detective Stevie Jorgenson that kept him thinking of her.

He pushed open the wooden door, stepped inside, and was awed. The lunch crowd was large. He scanned the place as much to find a place to sit as locating the man who owned the Audi. Seeing him sitting at the bar, surrounded on both sides by patrons, Mac looked for a spot close to him, glanced at him again and realized that one of the patrons sitting next to him was Sage. Her usual long dark ponytail was now a dark knot at the crown of her head. Lucky day.

The smell of Ethan's chicken made his stomach growl, and even though he'd just had that chicken for supper last night, he'd likely have it again today for lunch. He made his way to the bar and gently squeezed Sage's neck as he sidled up next to her, his side to the bar, facing Sage and Audi man. He knew he was squeezing her in, but he wanted that spot when she took Levi his lunch.

"Hey, Mac. If I had known you'd be back for lunch, I'd have asked you what you wanted."

"No worries, Sage; I wouldn't have known until a bit ago." He watched the mysterious man. He seemed to be listening, without really listening. Then he turned and caught his gaze. Ethnic origins for sure. Deep brown eyes, almond in shape framed in thick dark lashes that would make any woman swoon. His rich tan skin was flawless. He wore a thick gold band on his right hand with an insignia on the side, though he couldn't see it clearly. The man nodded once then looked away.

Needing to stir up a conversation he said a bit loudly to Sage. "Did you see that Audi out front? Damn, but that's my dream car for certain."

Sage turned her head to him. "Really? I kind of had you pegged for a Camaro or Charger or something."

"I wouldn't turn those down either, but that sexy gal out front is a sight to behold."

He flicked his eyes to their quiet companion and back to Sage, and smart girl that she is, she smiled. "So, what do you think a car like that costs? Two hundred thousand or so?"

He chuckled. "Naw. Maybe a hundred thousand, and I supposed if a guy bought it used, he could get it for around eighty thousand or so. Maybe less."

Sage twisted her head and glanced around like she was looking for someone. Then, playing her part to perfection, she straightened and tilted her head to the well-dressed gentleman sitting next to her. "That your car out there?"

Looking down at her, a smile played on his lips. "Yes, ma'am, it is." His accent was definitely not from around here. Not a southern twang in it.

Picking up his glass, which looked like soda, he sipped. She leaned in as if she had a secret to tell and whispered, "You didn't pay two hundred thousand for that car out there. Did you?"

Studying her, Audi man's dark eyes roved her face then they tilted up to look at him. Nodding again, he set his drink on the coaster on the bar and held out his hand. "Estefan Sonatos." Shaking hands first with Sage then with him.

"Sage Reynolds." She tossed her thumb over her shoulder. "Sam McKenzie one of my partners."

"Partners?" Estefan's eyes traveled between the two of them, his brows high.

"We own Bluegrass Security. She glanced out the window then pointed. "We're right across the street."

Nodding, Estefan said, "Sure, we hired you to install the system out at Whispering Caves."

Keeping the surprise from his voice. "I thought you looked familiar and certainly your car does. I saw you there yesterday."

"Yes, you did. Nice setup you put together out there. Very impressive. My bosses will be pleased when I turn in my report."

Bosses. Interesting. "Where are you from? You don't sound like you're from around here."

Another soft smile. "Neither do you, amigo."

Amigo. Spanish. Estefan turned his body on the stool, so he was facing them. "I'm from the Chicago area, here to check a few things out. I'll be on my way in a day or two."

"So, the car is a rental? It has Kentucky plates on it."

The smile grew, and the man had perfectly straight, very white teeth. Everything about him screamed money.

"Something like that."

Ethan stopped in front of them with two bags of delicious smelling food. "Here you go, Sage. Hope you and Levi enjoy your first bite of my special chicken recipe." He placed the other bag in front of Estefan. "Anything else I can get for you today?"

Tossing a ten-dollar bill on the bar, he shook his head as he stood. "That's for you and no thank you. I'm good."

He reached for his lunch, nodded to them, and elegantly walked from the bar as they watched.

"What can I get you, Mac?"

Swiveling his head around, he grinned. "An order of your chicken and a bourbon. Your monthly blend."

"Sure thing."

Sage looked up at him. "What was that all about?"

Taking the newly-vacated seat, he leaned his elbows on the edge of the bar. "Let Levi know what just happened here, and he'll fill you in on the rest."

Sage picked up their lunch bag and scooted away quickly as she replied, "Okay. See ya back at the office."

12

Speeding along the country roads to her father's ranch, her home base, Stevie contemplated the upcoming conversation with her dad. She'd spent the past three days avoiding Mac, and now she was restless. She'd spent most of the last three days holed up either at the office or her apartment, and she was edgy. No pool shooting to ease her tension. No social interaction. And, sadly, no Mac. Which was stupid because that's what she was trying to do, right? Avoid the devilishly handsome man in her dreams?

She pulled up to Balmoral, and her mother was watering the potted flowers on the front porch. DeeDee Jorgenson was a beautiful woman—five-five, blonde hair, and blue eyes. She was the reason Stevie had the full breasts and round hips. Curvy was the polite term. Kids in school called her chunky. No matter how hard she worked out, she still had the boobs and the hips. As she stared at her mother, she knew she always would.

Wearing a tan straw hat to keep the sun from her skin, DeeDee gracefully advanced on her, arms extended to fold her oldest daughter in a hug before setting her back to keep her lipstick from smearing. She always wore lipstick. She kept it on her nightstand, and it was the first thing she put on in the morning. "I'd never let your daddy or anyone see me without my lips on. It just isn't ladylike to do so." The gentle southern accent would forever be imprinted on her brain, long after her mother was gone from this world.

"Stephanie, dear, you should cover your face from the harsh effects of the sun. You know how it can age you. Why, have you see Caroline Carlson lately? Good heavens, she looks to be twenty years older than she is." She began walking toward the house. "Truth be told, I'm a bit happy for it. What with her family they way they are and all."

And here it came, the litany of crimes the family had committed on the community, God, and everyone. And, they had done a fair amount, but over the years the tales grew longer and more horrific. Tuning it out, she glanced around for signs of her father. As if he knew she'd need to be rescued, he exited the front door and hurriedly walked to embrace her. His shoulders, which were usually upright and proper, slumped slightly forward. She swallowed the lump in her throat, seeing her hero looking slightly defeated.

"Stevie, so glad to see you. What brings this gift to our door?"

Squeezing her father, partly because she was happy to see him and partly because she was grateful for the rescue, she whispered in his ear, "I wanted to share some reports with you."

He stepped back at arm's length, his hands still on her shoulders and looked into her eyes. "Bad?"

She shrugged because she wasn't sure how he'd take some of this news.

"Okay then, let's go to the barn office." He ushered her toward the barn while calling over his shoulder, "We'll be back in a bit Dee. We'll sit and have a drink then, honey."

Stopping quickly at her Jeep, she reached in and pulled the folder carrying the reports she wanted to share with her father. He pulled his phone from his back pocket and tapped a couple of times, then held it to his ear. "My daughter is here with some reports about the happenings these past few days. Can you meet us in the barn office to take a look? I'd like your take on things."

Briefly glancing around for a vehicle, she didn't see anyone there. Must be Dan he'd called, but he would have used her name. The furrow in his brow was still there, the worry around his eyes deep set, and the clench in his jaw evident. The betrayal of having someone purposely poison an animal would no doubt make him want to kill. No one hurt an animal on Nicholas Jorgenson's watch.

He sat at the desk with a deep sigh, preparing himself for the information. She pulled up the chair against the wall behind him to sit alongside. Pulling the reports from the folder, she laid them in front of her dad.

"How's the mare?"

"Failing. Doc said she won't make morning."

She placed her hand on her dad's upper arm. "I'm sorry, Daddy."

He simply nodded and clenched his jaw tighter.

Pointing to the first report, she took a deep breath. "Oleander." She pulled two other reports from the folder and laid them next to the other. "Oleander in all three horses. There are a good ten miles between each of your farms, yet your horses found Oleander. And the farms in between haven't had any issues."

She pulled another paper from her folder. "This is a map of each of the three ranches who've had poisonings."

Footsteps approached, and a quick knock on the doorframe twisted her head to look into the deep dark eyes of the man she'd been trying to avoid this week. His eyes locked on hers and a slight shiver ran through her body. It was as if there were an electric current running between them. Every time she saw him, he brought her to life.

"Come on in, Mac, and take a look at what Stevie brought with her." He waved his hand over the reports. Quickly he added, "Oh, I'm sorry; Stevie honey, this is Sam McKenzie of Bluegrass Security. He installed a new system a couple of days ago and is here today to make a couple of adjustments. I wanted him to see this, so he knows what we're looking for during surveillance."

He walked toward her, and her nipples pinched. Dammit, it just wasn't fair. Her breathing deepened as his scent, still fresh despite the heat and time of day, floated over her and held on. If she closed her eyes, she could remember how it felt to be wrapped in his arms.

He leaned in close, picked up her hand in his, the roughened skin on his fingers sent a delicious shiver up her arm. He leaned forward. "We've met. Nice to see you again, Detective." He gently squeezed her hand, and dammit, she wanted him. It seemed simply impossible that he'd look even better today than when she first saw him, but he did. It seemed impossible that she'd risk growing attached, but she would. It seemed careless and irresponsible with her heart and totally dangerous to let go and enjoy what time she could with him. Right?

Her father cleared his throat, and she twisted her head and pulled her hand away from Sam's. She immediately wished she could sit here with her father and hold Sam's hand. Work with him, talk to him. Enjoy spending time with him.

Nicholas immediately began showing the reports to Sam, and he leaned in just over her right shoulder to look at the reports. His hip brushed her shoulder, and she shivered. If she turned her head toward him right now, she'd be looking. Right. There.

"Go on, Stevie." She blinked. Go on? Her father continued, "What's the significance of the map?"

She cleared her throat. Working to keep her voice even, she slowly responded. "The red stars are the three ranches where the poisonings have happened." She pointed. Removing a highlighter from the coffee cup that served as a pen holder on her father's desk, she quickly drew bright yellow circles around each of the ranches in between. "None of these ranches have been hit." Pulling another paper from the folder, she lay it on top of the maps. "This is a map of the area and the green marks are the ranches who have two-year-olds that could be contenders for next year's Derby." Of course, the three ranches that had been hit were Whispering Caves, Carlson's ranch, and two others. "Of the six in this close area, three of you have been targeted. Does that mean the other three will also be targeted?" She looked up at Mac as he leaned slightly over her and she didn't move away when his body pressed against hers. It felt ... fantastic. "Mac? Have you installed any systems on any of these other ranches besides Carlson's?"

He read the names on the map, Page and Irish Lady. "We've installed at the Page ranch; he was our first client."

"So, if I were a betting woman," pointing to the map, "we'd be wise to watch the Irish Lady to see if they are targeted next."

Her father looked at her, pride clear on his face. "I think you're right because they have two contenders for next year."

"Do we know what we're looking for yet?" Mac's rich, deep voice floated over her skin.

She pulled the first reports she'd lain on the desk forward. "Oleander. It's very poisonous to horses. They end up dying of heart failure. Doc Burgis confirmed that all three of the horses poisoned this week had it in their systems."

He stood, placed his hands on his hips and looked at the maps again. "Any idea how they are getting it?"

"None," she said, and she decided right there, as he brushed against her again to lean forward, that she needed to get him out of her system. Maybe that's all it was, just a thing that hadn't played out yet. That was probably it and now that she felt firm in that thought, her outlook improved, and the need and excitement clawed its way through her, suddenly eager to get this meeting over with.

"Stevie, I'd like Mac to have copies of these reports. Bluegrass is also doing surveillance of the property twenty-four-seven to keep any intruders out. Since they have systems at other ranches, it will help them in their jobs."

She smiled at her father. "Of course."

13

He'd been disappointed this week when on the two installs he did, Stevie didn't show up. He couldn't possibly assume she'd be on every install, but he enjoyed seeing her daily. Even when she was trying to ignore him, as she was now, just brushing up against her made him feel better. Alive. On fire. He liked that feeling. It had been forever since he'd felt like that.

Nicholas stood, his face still showed the signs of worry, but he could see the resemblance in his and Stevie's facial structure. Same nose, same cheeks, same smile. Then, her shape changed at the neck and down, and that was his favorite part. He could still remember what her full breasts felt like pushed against his heated skin.

"I'd better go and have that evening drink with your mother; she hates having her routine changed, and it'll likely be a long night for me. Stevie, you coming to join us?"

"No, Dad, I have work to do. I'll just give Mom a call later. Okay?"

She stood and embraced her father. He wrapped his arms tightly around her and kissed her temple. "Okay, darlin'. Mac, you're more than welcome to sit on the porch and have a drink with us."

"I appreciate it, Nick, but I need to finish up here and get back home to my pup."

Nick nodded, winked at his daughter and strode to the door. "Stevie, lock up when you leave; okay, honey?"

"I will, Daddy."

He rounded the corner and Stevie began gathering up the paperwork she'd brought. Tucking it into the folder, she stepped away from the desk. He halted her by stepping in front of her. She turned those crisp blue eyes up to his, and his heart skipped a beat. Running the backs of his fingers along her jaw, he watched her swallow. Slowly, he leaned in and kissed the skin beneath her ear, licked the same spot, and kissed his way up to her ear lobe, pulling it between his lips. She dropped the folder to the desk with a thud, reached forward with both hands and placed them on his hips. Placing his lips closer to her ear, he whispered, "I need you, Detective Stevie Jorgenson."

She mewled, and he just knew that those glorious nipples of her puckered. To make sure, he reached out with one hand and gently swiped his palm over her breast. The light green blouse she wore allowed him a thin layer of material between her nipple and his hand, and it felt fantastic. His cock throbbed to life. She let the air leave her lungs, and he reclaimed her lips. Holding her head between his hands, he turned her to fit his mouth perfectly, and he plunged his tongue in to taste her. Feel her. Be in her.

When his lips left hers to trail down the other side of her jaw, he heard her whisper in his ear. "Oh my God." Gooseflesh rose on his arms and back, and he quickly reclaimed her mouth, his hunger powerful.

He drove his hand into her hair and held her in place, his lips on hers, tasting her mouth, feeling her body against his. He tightened his arm around her waist and pulled her close, driving his hardness into her. A moan from deep within her throat left her and entered him, and he thought he'd explode. He tore his lips from hers and touched his forehead to hers while measuring his breathing. "I repeat. I need you, Stevie."

"Yes." It was a soft whisper, but he heard it.

"My place. Now."

She pulled away just enough to look into his eyes. "I thought you had work to do here."

"I lied. Didn't want to drink with your parents. No offense."

She smiled, stepped back, and crossed her arms in front of her—more protective than irritated. "Mac." The look on her face seemed pained; she looked to the ground and back to his chest, not looking into his eyes. His stomach clenched.

He tucked his fingers under her chin and pulled her face up, so her eyes met his. "Say it." He knew she wasn't married or otherwise involved. Levi and Sage's research told him that and so much more. She hadn't been with any other man for three years or so. She wasn't the slut he'd initially worried she was. Still, this look on her face sent off warning bells of epic proportions.

She cleared her throat. "Mac, I can't have babies. If that's what you're interested in – in your future, I mean. I can't give you that. And, I don't want to get wrapped up in you if you're just going to break my heart."

He stared at her, the meaning clear and yet not. What in the hell?

"Stevie, why would you think I wanted you to give me babies. First of all, we haven't even been on a proper date, let alone family planning." He kept his voice even, but his body tensed.

She swiped her fingers down her face. Likely an effort to wipe away the worry. She dropped her hands to her sides and looked into his eyes. "My last boyfriend of three years dumped me when we found out I can't have children. He smashed my heart. Killed my confidence. Made me feel inferior." Her eyes glistened. "I can't do that again. I thought it best you know right away."

"Oh, honey." He stepped forward and wrapped his arms around her, pulling her close. Her hands hung at her sides for a long time, but he didn't let go. He laid his cheek on the top of her head and he heard her sniff. When it felt as though she'd relaxed in his arms, he leaned back to look at her. "I'm sorry. I can't imagine strong, confident Stephanie Jorgenson—detective extraordinaire—could be shaken to her core." He touched his thumb and forefinger to her chin and looked her firmly in the eye. "I'm not sure what makes you think I want babies; frankly, the thought of starting a family at my age panics me." He took a breath, settling the anger that threatened to rise at the asshole who made this beauty ever feel as though she were less. "I'd given up the thought of having my own children a long time ago."

"But ..." She licked her lips and swallowed again. "You call Ammo your baby. I thought it meant that ..."

He stared at her as her words and the realization that she had been running from the fact that she thought she couldn't give him something she thought he wanted flew through his mind. Damn.

Softly he explained. "I get that from my dad. He taught us that animals are so reliant on us, as if we're their parents. The responsibility of having a pet is total. They are our children, requiring our attention, housing, food, protection, medical needs, we owe them that if we take the responsibility of having a pet. My dad called every dog we ever had as I grew up, Baby. He said us boys would grow and move away; his babies didn't."

Her damp lashes blinked several times, and her face softened.

"Really?"

He chuckled. "Really."

Then, she said the most amazing thing. "Your place. Now." Perfect.

14

The drive to Mac's gave her time to process all that had just happened. Relief flooded through her at his explanation about why he called Ammo his baby. And wasn't that sweet? His family's deep love of animals mirrored her family's love and livelihood. Animals were their business. They spent thousands of dollars a year in veterinarian care for their horses' feed and housing.

The fact that he wasn't bothered by her inability to have children further made her feel soft and squishy. She'd been feeling so bereft for so long and quite frankly, inadequate, that she'd failed to see that children didn't mean everything to everyone. She actually giggled at this new found information.

She hit the Bluetooth connection and said, "Call Tina."

A few beeps and clicks and the robotic repetition of her command, followed by the ringing of the line stopped after the second ring. "Hey, Stevie, how did it go?"

Tina, her assistant at the office, knew most everything about her, and on top of that, she was efficient, smart, and so damned reliable.

"It went better than anticipated. I'm giving my reports to Sam McKenzie of Bluegrass Security. Can you make sure the scanned copies are emailed to me and uploaded to my cloud file? I may need them later this evening as I go over them."

"Sure thing." Tapping on the other end. "Done. By the way, I had the extreme pleasure of seeing Sam McKenzie leaving the grocery store yesterday. He was carrying a fifty-pound bag of dog food, and he made it look easy. He's fine. I actually stopped and gaped at him, then Marcy, the clerk at the store, said they just love when he comes shopping. Every woman in the store had stopped shopping and watched him walk out the door. Then, if you listened closely, there was a collective sigh."

She smiled. If Tina only knew. "Yes, he's certainly fine. He's also smart and wait till you hear his voice. Think Sam Elliot."

"Ohh, I'm fanning myself here. Maybe I need a security system installed at my place."

She smiled and was grateful the pink in her cheeks couldn't be seen through the connection. "See you tomorrow. Have a great night, Tina."

She tapped the *End Call* icon and continued following the lady magnet's truck to his place, the excitement making this ride seem like forever!

Pulling alongside his truck under the carport beside his house, she glanced around for Ammo to come bounding out of his door. She pulled a treat from the bag in her glove box and jumped from her Jeep, reports in hand.

Mac whistled, "Ammo, come on boy." His eyes were scanning the area. He looked to her, his hand outstretched for her to take, and she gladly ate up the distance between them. "It's not like him not to come outside and greet me." He pulled her to the kitchen door, unlocked it, and stepped inside pulling her with him. "Ammo? Come on, boy."

Silence. Mac tossed his keys in a small wooden bowl on the counter filled with change, a paper clip, and now his keys. His brows raised when he looked at her and he walked to the back of the house. She followed, not sure what to do.

"Ammo. Come on, baby, what's going on?"

She rounded the corner to what was clearly his bedroom and Mac glancing at Ammo's bed on the floor but no Ammo.

His worried face turned her way. "I have to go and find him."

He brushed past her out the door and down the hall; she stayed close behind. "We'll go together." She tossed the reports on the counter at the same time Mac pulled his keys from the bowl. Out the door they went and quickly walked to the water's edge, both calling out for Ammo.

Stevie's detective radar went up, and she began searching

the shrubbery and nooks and crannies along the lake's edge where a pup could crawl.

Nothing. Not even tracks.

Together they began walking down the driveway searching in the longer grasses alongside. Mac's voice was beginning to take on the panicked high pitch of a person who was beginning to think the worst.

They walked to the end of the driveway until it met up with the road, about a half-mile and no sign of the pup. They turned to walk back, and she wracked her brain. Where would he go? He had a collar on, free reign on coming and going, food and water.

"Let's go back to the truck and drive down the road." His worried voice touched her deep within.

"Okay. Let me call the office and ask the patrol officers to keep a look out too." She didn't wait for a response, just pulled her phone from her pocket and tapped the icons needed to dial.

Upon hearing Tina's voice, she quickly told her of the situation and asked that she have dispatch relay the story and be on the lookout. It was a long shot, but at least she felt as though she was doing something.

They climbed into Mac's truck, and she hung her head from the window, scanning the area for any signs of the pup. About a mile from Mac's driveway, he came to an abrupt stop in the road. She turned her head to glance out his window just as he jumped from the driver's seat. There lay a lump of black and tan fur. She raced around the truck to kneel down beside Mac and an injured Ammo.

His breathing was shallow; blood covered his mouth and fur. His paws were scraped and raw; his knee joints were as well. Mac softly touched Ammo's face and crooned soft words to comfort him. She saw the tears gather in his eyes.

She touched his arm softly. "Mac. You need to pick him up and carry him to the truck. You hold him, and I'll drive to Doc Burgis' clinic."

His wet eyes locked on hers and her heart broke. She didn't look away and silently willed strength and knowledge to come their way. His sadness killed her.

He finally nodded once. "Sorry, boy, this might hurt, but we've got to get you some help."

Ammo yelped as Mac picked him up, but he held him close as he slowly walked to the pickup. She opened the passenger door and helped him step up into the truck while trying their best not to jostle Ammo. Once he was in and the pup seemed settled, she softly closed the door and hurried around to the driver's side. As soon as she had the seat adjusted and the truck in gear, she pulled her phone out and called Doc Burgis.

The good doctor met them in the parking lot with a smaller gurney, perfect for large animals, not big enough for a human. Mac gently laid Ammo on the gurney, though he struggled at the loss of his master holding and calming him.

"Keep your hand on him so he can feel you and keep talking to him. We'll slowly roll him in, so he doesn't become frightened and try to jump." Doc was efficient and calm.

Running ahead to open the door her heart raced as Ammo's lethargic body and shallow breathing worried her. Though he squirmed occasionally, he listened to Mac's soothing words.

Once in the examination room, Doc quickly went to work. She gave him a shot to calm him while she examined his wounds, took pictures, wrote data on her chart. He had some gashes that needed stitches. She took blood samples from the blood in his mouth, which she quickly handed off to her assistant, Nicole, a gorgeous Hispanic woman in her late twenties. She had luxurious thick dark hair, an angelic face and the compassion for animals any veterinary assistant would require. A couple knots of jealousy punched her gut when Nicole looked at Mac and reassured him they'd help Ammo. Mac's grateful smile clawed at her insides just a bit. Then, realizing the situation, she calmed herself down and thanked God Ammo had Mac, Nicole, and Deanne Burgis to save him.

Two hours later, Ammo was patched up and resting peacefully, and she was sitting in the room with him and Mac as Deanne finished looking at the lab data. Mac's hand never left Ammo's coat, touching him where a bandage or abrasion wasn't and he often watched his pup's face for signs of distress, but none came. His other hand had grabbed hers, and as the thoughts of what may have happened rolled through her brain, he'd squeeze her hand, or she'd squeeze his. Just that movement said so much; they spoke very little.

"Thank you." His deep sexy voice floated over her like a warm blanket. She looked up into his gorgeous eyes, still filled with worry and confusion, and her heart pattered a bit faster.

"No need to thank me. I'm glad to be here with you."

He squeezed her hand again then looked at Ammo.

Deanne softly entered the room and pulled the rolling stool over to sit in front of them, her file on Ammo in front of her. Her copper hair—still pulled into the ponytail she always wore—shined where the last rays of the sun shone through the window. She pulled the file open and pointed to a lab result.

"The blood in Ammo's mouth was human. We tested it because he doesn't have any cuts or abrasions near his mouth, yet there was a fair amount of blood in it. My guess is someone tried to steal him. Maybe they manhandled him which would explain the bruising around his neck and the break in his front left leg. If I look at his injuries, I'd say they got him into the car and started driving. Maybe trying to hold him still is how his leg was broken, he turned and bit his attacker and then either jumped or was thrown from the vehicle. The break in his leg isn't surrounded by abrasions like he'd broken it hitting the ground, but the other scrapes and cuts are indicative of a fall and scraping on the road. Road rash." She glanced at him and smiled sweetly. "He'll be fine in a few days. He may need to wear a cone if he licks at his wounds, and the cast can come off his leg in two weeks."

Mac nodded. "Thank you, Doc, I appreciate all you've done for Ammo."

"My pleasure. I'd say the man you're looking for, assuming you'll be looking," glancing at Stevie, then back to Mac, "has a nasty bite on his hand or arm and probably needs stitches. I've called it in to the police department and the hospitals as required by law."

Deanne stood and extended her hand to Mac. "Please bring him by tomorrow for a follow-up, no need to keep him overnight."

Mac shook her hand and nodded. "I'll bring him in the morning."

Handing him a prescription bottle with some white pills in it, she added, "He'll need these for the next four or five days for the pain. Once he's up and walking around, the first day or so especially, you'll need to try and keep him calm. No running or jumping. When you go to work, lock his doggy door. Other than that, he should do well."

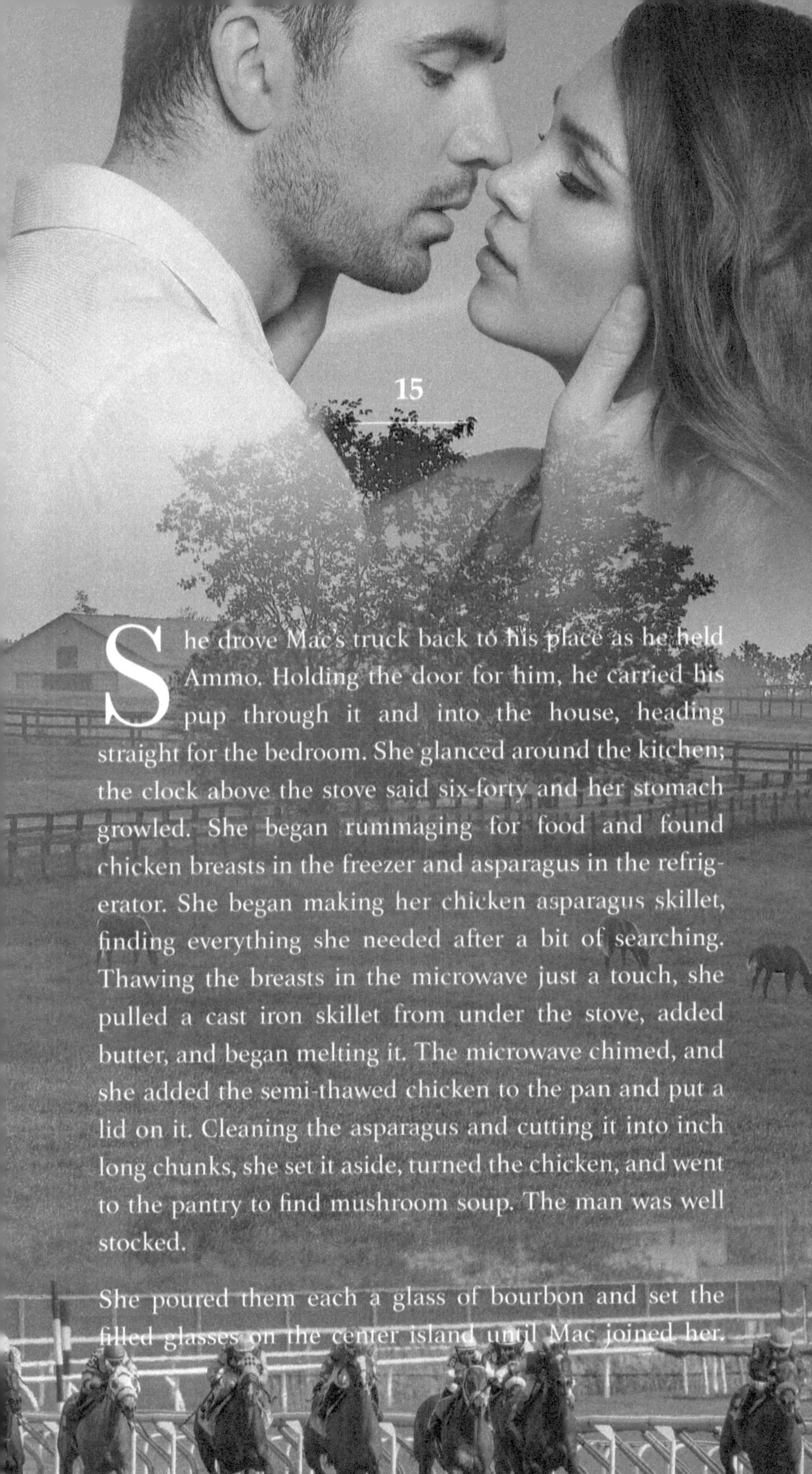

15

She drove Mac's truck back to his place as he held Ammo. Holding the door for him, he carried his pup through it and into the house, heading straight for the bedroom. She glanced around the kitchen; the clock above the stove said six-forty and her stomach growled. She began rummaging for food and found chicken breasts in the freezer and asparagus in the refrigerator. She began making her chicken asparagus skillet, finding everything she needed after a bit of searching. Thawing the breasts in the microwave just a touch, she pulled a cast iron skillet from under the stove, added butter, and began melting it. The microwave chimed, and she added the semi-thawed chicken to the pan and put a lid on it. Cleaning the asparagus and cutting it into inch long chunks, she set it aside, turned the chicken, and went to the pantry to find mushroom soup. The man was well stocked.

She poured them each a glass of bourbon and set the filled glasses on the center island until Mac joined her.

She pulled her phone from her pocket, tapped her music icon and began playing a bit of the Zac Brown Band. She lay her phone alongside the bourbon glasses and turned to the stove. She added the soup and asparagus to the skillet and reached to place the cover on top when strong arms wrapped around her waist and a hard body settled up against her back. His scent swirled around her, that fresh cleanness that was forever imprinted on her soul. His lips kissed the top of her head then slid to her ear, and his deep, sexy voice softly crooned. "Thank you for taking care of us." He kissed just behind her ear and her nipples puckered. She topped the skillet and wrapped her arms around his.

"You don't have to thank me. Ever." Turning to face him, her hands went to his face, her thumbs swiping away the worry under his eyes. Staring into the deep brown orbs, she knew she was lost. It was kind of silly of her to think she wouldn't even try to get to know this man. The instant she laid eyes on him, something changed in her. She gently pulled his face to hers and placed a gentle kiss on his lips. One turned to two, and two turned to many more. When his tongue slid into her mouth, she whimpered and held his head firmly in place, loathe to let him go.

Man, he was good at kissing. His soft lips always melted over hers just perfectly, claiming her without bruising or roughness. His tongue always sought hers, danced with hers, and she marveled at how she'd already grown accustomed to the feel of his mouth on her. And how instinctively she just knew what he was going to do next.

His hand slid around and cupped her breast, squeezing just so before grasping her nipple between his thumb and forefinger and squeezing harder. Shot. Straight. To. Her. Pussy.

Sliding her hands down to cup his fine ass, she pulled him to her and swallowed the groan he emitted from deep within his throat. Exciting.

"How long we got?" His words were clipped in between kisses.

"What?" She leaned back and blinked.

"How long?" He nodded to the stove. "Before it's ready?"

Oh.

"Um ... twenty minutes."

"Not enough."

She shook her head slightly. "Yeah, that'll be enough."

"No. It won't."

He unbuttoned her top two buttons, reached his big hand into her bra and pulled out a breast, quickly leaning down to suck her nipple into his mouth. He suckled, nipped, and suckled more until she was panting. "Won't be enough time to do everything I want to do to you."

Oh.

Wow.

He swiped his work-roughened thumb over her wet nipple, and a hard shiver traveled the length of her body. At this rate, her panties would be drenched.

He stepped back and tucked her boob back into her bra, buttoned her two buttons and kissed her forehead. He turned to the counter picked up both glasses of bourbon and handed her one.

"I'm gonna need a long time." He tapped his glass to hers and swallowed down a healthy mouthful never looking away from her.

Wow.

She drank down a nice amount, closed her eyes as the burn made its way all the way down. Loved that feeling.

He chuckled, and she opened her eyes to see him staring intently at her. She cocked her head to the side.

"I love watching you enjoy a good drink of bourbon. And you do enjoy it. Not like these little wine sippers and lettuce eaters. It's sexy."

She scrunched her face. "Wine sippers and lettuce eaters?"

"Yeah." He pulled plates from the cupboard and walked to the table. "I've never dated anyone who would eat a damn good meal and drink a real drink. You do both. It's sexy."

Wow.

She sipped once again, let it slide then set her glass on the counter. "We're not dating."

"Yes, we are."

"Since when?"

"Since you told me why you were avoiding me, and I told you I didn't care. We've been dancing around each other for the past week or so, but I can't seem to get you out of my head, and I think I'm inside of yours too. Don't know how I know it, just do." He sipped again and leaned his fine ass against the counter. "Dating."

"Dating means you go out in public, have fun, do things together, et cetera."

"We've done things together. The best thing."

"Not what I'm talking about."

"Tomorrow night we'll go out. What do you want to do, shoot pool?"

"Can you leave Ammo here alone?"

"I'll see if Sage and Levi can come and sit." He smiled. "Date?"

She stared into his eyes for a long time. They were earnest and still so damned sexy, framed with thick full lashes. The little lines at the outer corners added that super sexy character and she admired them. She'd just had this conversation with herself; she couldn't deny it now. "Date."

"Tonight, though, we're going to do stuff. A lot of it."

Her heart hammered in her chest at the innuendo and excitement skittered through her body.

16

Slowly dragging Ammo's bed to the kitchen, he continued to speak softly to the pup so he wouldn't get freaked out. But, he didn't want him feeling like he was all alone in the room while they were out here eating. Plus, he was probably hungry. He rounded the corner from the hall and set Ammo's bed next to his dishes. He refilled the water and food and sat on the floor offering encouragement while Stevie prepared rice to go with dinner. He watched her as much as Ammo. Her sweet ass was moving and shaking as she made him dinner, without asking her to. She just saw it needed to be done and pitched in.

Glancing back at his pup, he was so grateful Ammo was alive and safe again and so grateful Stevie had been along with him when he found his little fur baby alongside the road. His stomach twisted at the pitiful sight of the bloodied clump of fur lying beside the road. Had she not been there, he would have freaked the fuck out – no lie. Part of him was able to stay in control because he didn't want to worry her. She was calm, took charge, drove, called Doc Burgis and making herself helpful at home.

"Is he eating?"

She'd walked toward them and squatted down next to them.

"Not yet. Doc said the pain pills might make him too tired to eat, but I wanted to make sure he knew he had food and water. Maybe when we go about eating, he will too. "

She smiled and looked into his eyes. "Okay. It's ready when you are."

He kissed her quickly because he just needed to at that moment, but he was anxious to get her naked right after supper. It'd been a long week. "I'm ready."

She stood and then held her hand down to help him up. He smirked but couldn't resist touching her, so he took her smaller hand in his and allowed her to tug lightly on his arm. When he was standing, he wrapped his arms around her waist and kissed her more completely, because he really wanted to do that.

Ammo had eaten a couple of bites and drank a bit of water. Once the dishes were cleared, Mac scooted the dog and bed to the bedroom. Stevie followed behind with Ammo's dishes, in case he was hungry later. Mac patted the pup on the head and turned to stare at this beautiful woman in front of him. She cocked her head slightly, and he thought it was the sweetest look he'd seen her wear.

"Take your clothes off, Peaches."

A slow smile spread her lips, her tongue peeked out then slid back in, and his cock jumped. "Peaches?"

He stepped toward her slowly, the thought of doing stuff with her the only thing on his mind right now.

"Yes. You're not moving your hands in the motions it takes to get that shirt off. Peaches." He smiled as he saw the blush tint her cheeks.

Finally, she began undoing those damned buttons. The first time he'd seen her do this, he thought he'd explode right there. He'd thought of it over and over this week. Her eyes never left his, though now she had to crane her neck up to keep the eye contact with him. He ran the backs of his fingers down her pink-tinted cheeks and felt the heat. He knew she had so much more of that heat in her.

She slowly let her blouse slide down her arms, and he broke the eye contact because he wanted to see her tits. They were fantastic. Firm. Round. Full. Perfect.

Even better, the quick rise and fall of her chest told him she was excited. Good news. "How about losing the bra too?"

Reaching behind her, she easily unhooked her bra, and as it slid down her arms, she caught it with one finger, held it to the side, and let it plop to the floor. He only saw a bit of scrap from the corner of his eye because his eyes were on her perfect tits. Seriously. They were perfect.

Right before his eyes, her nipples puckered to perfect points and his mouth watered. He dropped to his knees and sucked one of those glorious nipples into his mouth while eagerly grabbing the other one with his free hand. Squeezing and playing with it, the fullness making his cock harder than it'd been since his teen years when the damned thing was hard all the time.

Her taste in his mouth was sensual—if sensual were a taste. The aroma of peaches still surrounded her. It filled his senses now, but he had no explanation as to why she always smelled like peaches to him. Just did. He felt her fingers dig into his hair, massaging their way to the back of his head as she held him in place. Nope, that made his cock harder than it had been in years.

He kissed his way across her chest, swiping his thumb over the wet nipple he'd left and latching on to the warm, pliable one he'd been playing with. Damn. Perfect tits.

Hearing her moan and feeling the vibration against his lips excited him. His hand left her breast and joined his other hand as he unsnapped and unzipped her jeans, then tugged them down her rounded hips. His mouth never released her, even when her pants hit the floor with a thud, and she stepped out of them. His fingers felt the scrap of material that served as panties, and he thought, *what the hell*? A quick tug and he managed to rip the thin little strap that held the front to the back. The gasp from Stevie, then her laugh afterward, was worth it, and he'd buy her a dozen pair or more for that reaction. One last suck, then he let her nipple pop from his mouth so he could look at her.

"Gawd, that's sexy." Her slow southern drawl was more pronounced.

Letting the scraps fall to the floor, he admired the golden curls now presented before him. Her fingers moved in his hair, softly massaging his scalp, impatient for what would come next. Splaying his hands on her hips, his thumbs lightly circled through those sexy curls, slowly parting her moist lips for his tasting pleasure. Her breathing hitched and a smile played briefly on his lips as he dipped his head and swiped his tongue along the seam.

She gasped as his tongue found the precious little bud hidden within the softness. The texture against his tongue was like no other. As her juices flowed, her taste exploded in his mouth, and suddenly he felt like a starving man unable to get enough. He pulled her clit into his mouth, gently sucking, teasing it with his tongue before sucking again. Her legs began quivering, her moans growing louder.

He lifted his head and kissed his way up her belly before rocking back on his heels and looking up at her. The look of passion in her eyes, the softness of her face at this moment and the pliability of her body were burned on his brain—forever. The position of her head from his vantage point, between her gorgeous breasts, would be what he'd think about over the years. Stunning.

He stood, swept her off her feet, carried her to the bed and laid her down so quickly it didn't register on her face until he was leaning over her. He loved doing things with Stevie. She was easily lost in her passion, and it was glorious. Not worried about how she looked or if her tummy was perfect. She just jumped into the moment and enjoyed it.

Her eyes locked on his and her hand reached up to rest on his cheek, her soft fingers brushing away thought and worry.

"You're a sexy man, Sam McKenzie."

He chuckled. "You're a damn sexy woman, Peaches." He lightly kissed her lips before crawling down the bed, trailing kisses along the way, until he reached those sweet curls and the treasure she had within. The erotic moan she made when his mouth met her pussy and his tongue dipped in for more made his cock throb. Pulling her knees up, so her feet were resting on the bed, then gently pressing them open gave him access to the most alluring sight. Her moist, pink pussy opened to him, and he dove in to enjoy it. He occasionally stopped to glance at her face and momentarily enjoy the soft look her features took on—her eyes closed, her mouth open, her breasts moving as she bucked and writhed under his mouth. Glorious. He watched her face as he slid a finger into her channel and her mouth rounded into a perfect "o," then a soft smile as he slowly pulled out and slid back in. Then the second finger and he got the same look from her. That's what he'd remember as the days passed and he dreamt of her. Simply perfection.

He tasted her fully, enjoying the feel of her inside and out, and as her orgasm rapidly raced toward the finish line, the thought hit him that he needed to watch this happen. He continued massaging her with his fingers inside and tasted her with his tongue and lips, faster and harder until that moment when she exploded; then he lifted his head to watch her face in extreme pleasure. He was not disappointed.

She opened her eyes and locked with his, a soft smile on her lips. "I've got no words, Mac. That was simply ... everything."

He chuckled as he crawled his way up her body, kisses touching her body in various places. A deep suck on each breast then he looked into her eyes. "Might need some help, Peaches."

"Happy to oblige." She leaned up slightly to unsnap and unzip his jeans. He purposely didn't move; he wanted her to work for it. She seemed undeterred. Once she'd pushed his jeans as far as she could, she laid back and hooked her toes into the waistband and pushed them over his hips. He smiled as her progress unsheathed his cock and it bobbed out, touching the curls he'd just so lovingly tasted. That made his cock harder than it'd been since his teen years. It was that.

Moving one foot at a time, he kicked his jeans off slightly grimacing when they hit the floor with a thud. Stevie's fingers wrapped around his cock and pumped him, swirling her thumb over the top as she locked eyes with him. One hand reached down and palmed his balls, and he fought the urge to close his eyes. He wanted to watch her. Her pupils dilated, and her crisp blue eyes deepened into a sexy shade of ocean blue. He now had a new favorite color.

Pumping once more she guided his cock to her entrance and lifted her hips, wanting him to enter her. Her hands moved to his hips and pulled him down on her, causing him to enter, and they both groaned. He pumped into her, and she wrapped her legs around his hips, meeting him thrust for thrust.

"How's it gonna be tonight, Peaches? Fast or slow?"

She smirked. "Hard. I want to come hard."

"Good answer," he ground out as he began thrusting, meeting her hips stroke for stroke. This was the hardest his cock had ever been. No doubt about it this time.

Her body wrapped around his and held him tight. They were a perfect fit. He rotated his hips, and she closed her eyes and moaned loudly, her fingers dug into his ass as she pulled him into her harder. He reached back and looped her leg over his arm, which allowed him to slid in farther, and they both sighed at the feeling. He increased his pace. Sweat coated his skin and hers, and it felt fantastic. She cried out, "Mac!" Her fingers tightened on one side of his ass, her head threw back, and her body jerked. He slowed his pace just a bit through her orgasm but kept watching her and sliding into her wet, pulsing pussy. When her eyes opened, a soft smile creased her lips. "I've never come so hard. Awesome."

"My turn." He increased his pace, pounding into her. By the fourth stroke, he shoved himself into her and released a groan escaping his throat at the power behind his orgasm. After he'd spilled himself into her, he flopped down to the bed, holding himself up on his elbows. Her arms wrapped around his shoulders and pulled him all the way down on top of her. The cushion of her breasts between them, slippery from their exertion, made his cock twitch. Just a bit. No, that's what he'd remember for the rest of his days. That was epic.

Once he could move, he rolled to the side and laid on his back. He took her hand in his and bent his elbow, kissing the knuckles of her fingers before heaving out a long sigh. She rolled slightly toward him and tossed her arm over his chest. He moved his arm so he could hold her close to him and she lay her cheek on his shoulder and closed her eyes.

He kissed the top of her head and closed his eyes, the aroma of warm peach cobbler on his mind. He'd forever think of her whenever peaches and peach-related things were near.

A whimper from the corner drew his gaze to Ammo who rolled to his side and felt the pain of one of his injuries, but he settled in, his eyes closed in slumber.

"I have ice cream."

She kissed his chest and lifted her head. She rested her chin on her hand and looked into his eyes for long moments. Finally, in her sweet southern voice, she said, "That sounds perfect."

His heartbeat sped up, and he was unable to lose that connection with her, so he continued watching her face. His hand began roving over her ass, the dip between her hip and her rib cage, her soft, warm skin felt excellent under his fingers.

The muffled song, *Fishin in the Dark* by Nitty Gritty Dirt Band began playing. She smiled, "Typical Dad timing."

He watched her roll from the bed and fish through her jeans on the floor for her phone. The curves this woman had were simply perfection. Picking up her clothes, she strode out the door toward the bathroom as she said, "Hey, Daddy. What's up?" He heard the door close. That was his cue to get up, though he'd prefer to lie here and wait for her to come back for round two.

He got up, pulled a pair of workout shorts from his dresser drawer, and pulled his phone from his jeans. In the kitchen, he locked the doors to the outside, pulled bowls from the cupboard and ice cream from the freezer and began scooping them each a bowl. The sun was almost set, a red ball quickly dipping past the horizon all that was left of this day. Pretty damn good end to what was a pretty shitty day.

17

The warmth on her torso felt divine. Her body was incredibly rested and relaxed. She'd slept better last night than she had in such a long time. Slowly opening her eyes to the room, the sun streaming through the break in the curtain slanted across her belly warming her whole body. She stretched her arms and glanced over to see the dent in the pillow where Mac had slept, but no Mac. Lifting slightly, she looked to Ammo's bed, and there was no Ammo either. Early risers.

Able to assess the room that was the most personal to Mac, she eagerly looked around. The walls were painted an interesting tan and pictures of a man with a lengthy and full Army career were hanging on the walls, and sitting on the dresser. He was dressed in cammies in most of the pictures, at one base or another. In a few of them, he wore civvies. In most of the photos he was doing something—few of them were posed.

She rolled to her side and rested her head in her hand and looked at the pictures on the dresser. A younger Mac stood with a woman, dark like him, much shorter, but her smile was the spitting image of his or his was the perfect image of hers. His mom, no doubt. The man standing on the other side of the woman was about two inches shorter, broad shoulders, sandy brown hair, same smile, same eyes. He looked to be a bit younger than Mac.

Another picture was a mature couple, looked like the same woman as the other picture and an older man – his parents.

The nightstand held a charging pad for his phone, which he promptly told her to make use of and she smiled as she saw both of their phones laying side by side on the tabletop. She laid back into her pillow and recalled the memories of spending the night with him. She was losing her heart to this man, and it was scary. After being dumped by Derek, she'd put the idea of love out of her mind, thinking she wasn't worthy of it. Now she felt hopeful, and it felt good. Her dormant heart was coming alive. She stretched and sat up, scooted to the edge of the bed and reached for her clothing, pulling her jeans on. She had no underwear because Mac had destroyed them. She sighed at the incredibly hot memory. It was a first for her.

Settling her bra in place, her phone lit up signaling a text. She walked to the bedside table, glanced down and her heart stopped. Her stomach churned and threatened to turn over and spill its contents as she reread the text. Tears stung her eyes and gathered in the corners, and her nose began to run.

She stepped back from the offensive phone, grabbed her blouse from the floor and pulled it on, quickly buttoning the buttons. She grabbed her phone and hurriedly rushed down the hall and out the kitchen door. Mac was standing just outside the door, Ammo standing, his broken paw held off the ground, his fur shaved in spots, some of them marred with stitches. She stopped dead in her tracks, and the pup looked up at her and wagged his tail, hopping two times toward her. She knelt down to greet him, and he wished her a good morning by lapping her a few times with his tongue. "Good morning, boy. Glad to see you up and getting around a bit."

She brushed away the tears with her fingers before standing and then began walking to her Jeep.

"Where are you going?"

"Home."

"Home? Not saying goodbye; just going home?"

She cleared her throat and slowly turned to look at him. Mistake. Big mistake. The furrow in his brow and confusion on his face wrecked her escape plan and threatened to weaken her. Then she remembered the offensive text.

"You had me investigated?" Her teeth clinched together; her back was ramrod straight.

His brows shot up into his hairline. "I ..."

She pointed at him, anger roiling through her at the rate of a stampede. "You had me investigated? How. Fucking. Dare. You."

"Peaches," his voice pleaded.

"No!" she shouted. "Don't you call me that again."

She turned to her Jeep, jumped inside, and started the engine. She quickly glanced to make sure Ammo didn't follow her and sped down the driveway without looking into his face. "Jerk!"

Entering her apartment, she headed straight to the shower to wash his scent from her skin. She stood under the hot water and let her tears mingle with the water. Once she was cried out, she'd be good again. She should never have let her guard down. She dared to dream. Dared to hope. Well, she'd never do that again. Ever. Reaching for her shower soap and squirting some into her hand the aroma of peaches rose into the warm steamy air. She grabbed the bottle again, read the label. Peaches and Cream shower soap. Her best friend, Toni, had given her this soap because she usually just bought something from the grocery store. "I'm telling you, hon, once you start using something that smells so damned good and makes your skin feel so soft, you won't ever go back to that grocery store stuff."

She stared at the perfectly ripe peach on the label and her eyes filled with tears to the point she couldn't see the perfectly ripe peach on the label anymore. Placing the bottle back onto the little shelf in her shower, she broke down into a good hard cry. She decided to let the tears flow.

Tapping the keys on her laptop, Stevie read the next report on the poisoning. It seemed the same variety of Oleander was used, meaning they'd gotten it from the same person or source. It had to be a person, and her mind instantly floated to Evanston Carlson. Her jaw clenched, and she flopped back into her kitchen chair blowing a breath from her lungs. "This sucks."

She jumped from her chair and walked to her refrigerator, opening the door and looking inside. "Shit." She'd not had the time to shop this week with all of the happenings in Bourbonville and the poisonings. She refused to think about Mac. She closed the door and picked her phone off the counter. She tapped the microphone. "Call Toni."

"Calling Toni." She walked to her living room and sat down. She glanced over the back of the soft gray, plush pile sofa she'd just purchased this winter, out the window onto Backstreet and the little houses that served as decorations to that street. Most of them white, each held an array of colorful baskets of varying shapes and sizes brimming over with gorgeous flowers of many varieties and in various stages of bloom. Her best friend Toni lived down Backstreet a ways, in one of those cute little white houses with baskets full of flowers. Her house was also filled with kids and toys and laughter.

"Hey, hon, what's up?"

At hearing her friend's voice, a sob caught in her throat. "Ton ... do you have a minute to talk to me?" She sniffed, and the tears threatened once again.

"Aww, honey. Of course, I do. Do you want to come down? I just put on some tea; it's a new brand."

She sniffed and cleared her throat. "I'll be right there."

She tapped the *end call* icon and swiped at her face once more. Walking into her bathroom, she checked her eyes in the mirror. There was no hoping she could hide the red rims and the puffy circles under them, so she shrugged, pocketed her phone, and slipped on her cute white sandals. Closing the door behind her, she exited at the front of her garage, which opened right onto Backstreet. The air smelled good here with the laundromat in full motion this morning. Saturday was the busiest day for it. A smile lifted her lips; to her, it meant she was making some extra money.

It was a sultry ninety degrees today, and she'd opted for a white gauzy tank and pink short shorts. Her legs were probably a bit thick for short shorts, but she liked them, and Toni told her she looked hot in them, so she put them in her cart and followed Toni to the lingerie section of the store. Shopping with Toni was a whirlwind. She seldom had time for anything, and a girls' shopping trip was usually a quick tour of the store, get the necessities and get out, so there was time for a couple drinks. That was fine with her; shopping wasn't her favorite thing to do anyway.

The fragrances of the various flowers as she passed by welcomed her. Some of the homes' occupants were sitting on their covered front porches, ceiling fans blowing on them. She waved to each person she saw, and they all waved back. By the time she reached Toni's house, she felt a bit better and ready to talk about her broken heart and pissed-off-ness.

She tapped once on the screen door, opened it up, and stepped inside. It was oddly quiet for a house with three kids. "I'm in the kitchen," a friendly voice called to her, and she skirted the little table just inside the door which held a little bouquet of fresh flowers and a lip balm. Just past the living room was the sunny yellow kitchen drenched in light, neat as a pin and smelling wickedly good.

Her best friend poured two cups of tea and turned to set them on the table as she entered the room. Their eyes locked and Toni quickly set the teacups on the table and skirted around it, arms outstretched. "Aww, honey, tell me what's up." Warm, strong arms wrapped her in a cocoon as her bestie's head rested against hers. She smelled good, like hyacinth and bread. Her figure was full, her disposition warm, and her friendship valued more than anything she'd ever own. Toni had been with her through thick and thin—from middle school through today and beyond.

Proud of herself for not crying, she pulled away and began. "I met someone. Tall, dark, devilishly handsome, kind, sexy, excellent lover, loves his dog, and doesn't care that I can't have babies."

Toni sat at the table and motioned for her to do the same. As she picked up her teacup and sipped, tears stung her eyes. She set her cup down. "Is this peach tea?"

"Yes, isn't it yummy? Al's mom bought it for me." Cocking her head, she continued. "You're crying over my tea? Aww, honey, what's up?"

Taking a calming breath, she blew it out and sipped her tea. It was yummy. Toni's mother-in-law had great taste.

"I think I fell hard for him and then I found out this morning that he had me investigated."

Toni's head popped up then cocked to the side and studied her face. "You mean as in investigated like did you ever commit a crime investigated?"

All she could do was nod.

"Why?"

She shrugged and shook her head. "Don't know."

"Well, what did he say when you asked him?"

She frowned. "I didn't."

Toni sat back in her chair and crossed her arms over her ample bosom. "You didn't ask him? Shit, honey, that'd be the first thing out of my mouth. What did you say to him?"

Swiping her brows with her fingers, she let out a long breath. "I just threw the accusation at him and he didn't deny it."

"What? He just said yeah, so what?"

"No." She sat back and blew out a long breath—again. She rotated her head and rolled her shoulders back. "I guess I didn't give him a chance. I was getting dressed and saw my phone light up that I had a text, so I walked over to the bedside table, and it was his phone. His partner, Levi, texted and said, *I have the investigation completed on Detective Jorgenson.* I flew out of the room and outside and shouted, he stammered, and I left."

Palms down on the tabletop, the warm peach tea floated up to her nostrils, and she inhaled. It did smell amazing. Her stomach growled. The oven timer went off, and Toni stood and pulled on an oven mitt. She turned to her, held her bright red mitt in the air and waved it. "I got this for fifty cents at Handy Andy's yesterday. Isn't it cute?"

She quickly turned and pulled fresh biscuits from the oven.

Her stomach growled again, and the perfect plate of biscuits slid in front of her was like salvation to a sinner. Toni went to the fridge, pulled out a jar of fresh homemade jam, swiped the butter from the counter, and set both in front of her. Bustling to the cupboard, she brought two plates, two knives, and two napkins, then sat across from her and nodded for her to go ahead. Quick, efficient, and awesome.

The warm biscuits on her fingers felt fabulous. Soft and airy, the warm brown bread made her mouth water. When she smeared the butter on it, and it instantly melted, the words *died and gone to heaven* floated through her mind. Toni's homemade biscuits were the best. A layer of strawberry jam and her first bite was as sensual as making love to Mac. She savored the different tastes as they exploded in her mouth then she enjoyed watching Toni take a big bite, close her eyes and moan.

They ate in silence for a few minutes. Toni's biscuits were to die for.

Swallowing, Toni washed her biscuit down with her warm tea. "The way I see it is like this. You need to ask him why he investigated you. And after you know that, then you decide what to do."

She was pierced with a set of vibrant green eyes and a stern set jaw. Nobody crossed Toni.

Softly, she said. "Okay."

Another bite of her biscuit and a splash of tea later Toni continued. "Now, tell me all about Mr. Tall Dark and Handsome. Don't leave anything out."

18

S tevie stormed off down the driveway and out of sight. Feeling helpless and quite frankly stunned, all he could do was watch. He dragged his hand through his hair and then down his neck and blew out a breath.

Ammo whined, and he glanced down to see his pup looking tired. Poor boy. He slowly walked to the back door to see if Ammo would follow. Taking longer than usual, but making headway, he allowed his pup to take his time; it was the only way he'd get stronger. As soon as they were in the house, Ammo drank some water then limped off to the bedroom. Following behind him, he entered the bedroom and picked up his phone. Tapping a couple of buttons and scrolling once, he found the offensive text message from Levi, read it twice then tossed his phone on the bed, flopping back next to it. Not how he'd hoped this morning would begin.

Staring at the ceiling, his mind filtered through several scenarios that would make this situation better. Honestly, nothing seemed adequate at this point. His phone rang, and he grabbed it up looking at the readout. Levi. Swiping the answer call icon, he put the phone to his ear. "I thought I asked you to be discreet."

Silence, then, "I was discreet."

"No, you weren't. You texted me telling me the investigation on Detective Jorgenson was complete, and she saw the fucking text. Why would you ever text something like that? Just leave the damned report for me in my basket at the office. It wasn't an emergency. Christ, Levi." His fingers rubbed the throbbing in his forehead, and his eyes closed.

Two hours later he strode into the office, still irritated and still with no answers as to how to fix things with Stevie. Levi was waiting for him, a sheepish set to his brows.

"I'm sorry, Mac. I didn't know she'd be there. It was 6:45 a.m. Who knew?"

He walked past his friend and went to the wire baskets on the counter along the upstairs coffee station where they each had in-baskets. The sealed manila envelope was on top of his basket, and he reached for it. Holding it in his hands, he felt a small stack of papers inside and nothing else. His fingers squeezed a few times but his stomach twisted at what this meant. Heaving out a long sigh, he turned and strode to the stairs; he'd go over to her place and apologize. Maybe they could resume this weekend on a positive note.

He nodded to Levi as he hit the top step. "Discreet means you don't give away secret things via text message. That also goes for voicemail and email."

He didn't lose his temper often, and normally this wouldn't have been a big deal, but it fucked things up with Stevie, and that sat hard. What he'd realized as he woke up this morning was he wanted to be with her. He wanted to explore a relationship with her. He enjoyed her company. Now, he didn't know if that would ever be.

Walking across the vacant lot between The Brass Rail and Sadie's Sweets, the freshness in the air mellowed him. The laundromat was in full swing, and the whole area smelled like clean clothes, fabric softener, and hope; no wonder she liked living above a laundromat, but it sure didn't fit with her family situation. Her parents lived on a sprawling ranch surrounded by award-winning horses, and the blue-green grass Kentucky was known for.

He stopped in front of her white door, turned the knob only to find it locked. Looking around for a doorbell and finding none, he turned and looked around the building for another entrance. Next to the door leading into the laundromat was another white door matching the back door. Twisting the knob, this one was also locked. Knocking loudly, he yelled, "Stevie, it's Sam. Can we talk?"

He waited, hearing nothing. Continuing to look around for a doorbell or an intercom, he made a note to find out who the landlord of this property was. Should be some way to notify the upstairs tenant someone was here. He pulled his cell phone from his pocket and dialed her number. No answer. He decided against a voicemail, tucking his phone into his pocket and walking back to his truck. The song, *Rebel Soul*, from Kid Rock began playing on his phone. Pulling it from his pocket, he answered. "Levi, not now."

"Wait, Mac; this is important. I got a couple of hits on the plates you wanted me to run on that Audi."

"I'm just out front; I'll be right up." Trying to clear his mind of all things Stevie, he entered the building to Regina pouring herself a cup of coffee.

"Mornin' Mac, ready for another busy day?"

Her smile was large and bright. "Yeah. Business is booming these days."

She giggled. "Good news, right?"

"Yeah." He turned up the steps and made his way to the office Levi shared with Sage. He was still sore at his friend, but in truth, he shouldn't have had her investigated in the first place. That much was clear to him now, so he couldn't completely fault Levi.

Levi turned one of his computer screens toward him. "Plates are registered to RRI, as in Roberto Rocelli International. Rumor has it Rocelli has mob ties. That is, his father is Don Rocelli." He looked at the information on the screen and Levi scrolled down a bit. A photograph of Roberto Rocelli appeared.

"That's not the man I saw driving the car."

Levi scrolled further. Another picture appeared on the screen. "Nope, not him. Said his name is Estefan Santos."

Levi tapped his name into the computer, and they waited as information began scrolling onto the screen.

"Estefan Santos, thirty-two years old, Bachelor's degree in Business Administration, one-time hip-hop hopeful, and now employed by RRI."

Processing the information, he said, "Check into the business ventures of RRI. I saw a stall in the barn at the Carlson ranch with the RRI logo on it. It looked like feed, and I asked Chuck and Dirks to watch that stall to see what type of activity was going on in there. If it's feed, it's separated from the other feed, which is in a grain barn out back. And, I saw Santos leaving the Carlson home. In that car. Something's going on there."

Walking to the door, Levi asked, "Where are you going?"

"Out to the Carlson ranch to have a look around and see what I can see."

"You don't have the right to trespass, Mac."

"Not going to. Paying a visit. I think one of the cameras isn't working." He stopped in his office to grab his laptop. As he passed Levi's office, he poked his head into the room. "Can you have Dirks back me up on the cameras? Specifically, the stall in the barn." He slipped out the back door and made his way to the Carlson ranch.

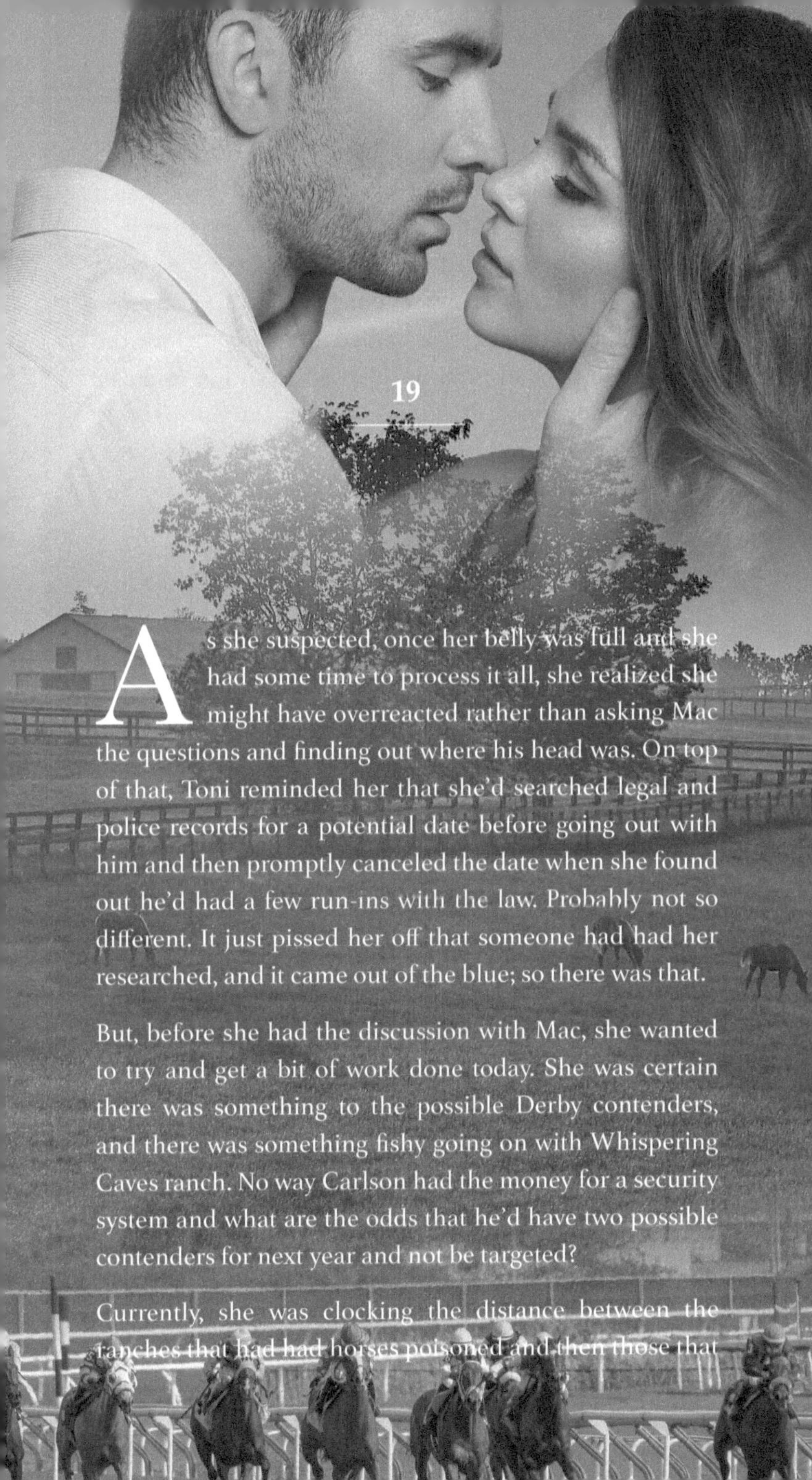

19

As she suspected, once her belly was full and she had some time to process it all, she realized she might have overreacted rather than asking Mac the questions and finding out where his head was. On top of that, Toni reminded her that she'd searched legal and police records for a potential date before going out with him and then promptly canceled the date when she found out he'd had a few run-ins with the law. Probably not so different. It just pissed her off that someone had had her researched, and it came out of the blue; so there was that.

But, before she had the discussion with Mac, she wanted to try and get a bit of work done today. She was certain there was something to the possible Derby contenders, and there was something fishy going on with Whispering Caves ranch. No way Carlson had the money for a security system and what are the odds that he'd have two possible contenders for next year and not be targeted?

Currently, she was clocking the distance between the ranches that had had horses poisoned and then those that hadn't and then the distance between all of them. The roads in Chandler County were curvy and hilly which added to the beauty of the area but could be treacherous if not careful. She rounded the final corner to Whispering Caves and glanced at her odometer. Exactly five miles from the Page ranch. She pulled over just before the driveway in a small turnout to write down her findings. Glancing down the driveway, she saw an Audi slowly making its way toward the road from the drive. She jumped from her Jeep and opened the back hatch. She had a blanket, flares, and of course her spare tire.

The Audi turned onto the road and headed toward her. She stepped back from her Jeep and looked down at the rear tire on the driver's side. The Audi slowed, and the driver's window rolled down.

"You need help, Miss?"

Looking the man in the eyes, she shrugged. "I thought one of my tires was flat, but they seem just fine, but the Jeep felt like it pulled so I thought it better to pull over and take a look."

"You need to make a call or need a lift somewhere?"

"No, thank you. I've got my cell, and my boyfriend is on his way." She closed the tailgate. "Nice car. Not too many of those around here."

He smiled at her, and her heart fluttered a bit. He was handsome in an exotic sort of way—perfect smile, burnished flawless skin. "I've been hearing that a lot. If you think you're okay, I'm going to move on."

She waved. "Thank you. I'm fine."

He pulled away and just as she turned to get into her Jeep, a white pickup truck advertising Bluegrass Security pulled alongside her. The window lowered. "Everything okay?"

She wrinkled her nose then placed her hands on her hips. "Of course."

He nodded and backed his truck up to park behind her. She took a deep breath and watched as his long legs dropped from the driver's seat and strode toward her. The look on his face seemed almost hesitant, but his eyes sought hers, and just before he stopped in front of her she saw his chest rise and heard the slow exhale. He was nervous too. It made her feel more secure for some reason.

"I owe you an apology, Peaches. I'm sorry."

Her heart hammered in her chest. Never had a man looked her in the eye and apologized. Wow. She stared into his eyes and only saw honesty. Her throat dried and she swallowed, then her nose tingled signaling tears. Gawd, she'd had enough of that today. She cleared her throat but wasn't sure what she should say. Then he reached forward and took her hand in his, wrapping his fingers tightly around hers and pulling it up to kiss the backs of her fingers. Wow.

"I'm sorry too." Her voice cracked, and she swallowed. "I should have stayed and talked to you, but my feelings were hurt, and I lashed out."

He tugged her hand around his waist pulling her firmly into his body, his arms securing her in a warm, comforting hug. She laid her head on his chest and listened to his strong, rapid heartbeat. She squeezed him tighter, and her heart felt lighter.

Pulling back, she looked up into his handsome face. "What are you doing out here?"

He glanced toward the ranch and took a deep breath. "I needed to go and check some things out at the ranch."

"Oh, bad equipment or something else?"

He hesitated, his mouth turned down. "Mac, is there something going on with Evie?"

He looked into her eyes and indecision seemed to play on his face. "Mac, don't hold back. Maybe we can work on this together. I need to solve these poisonings so no more horses are hurt."

She exhaled loudly and scraped her hands through her hair. "I know there must be something going on at this ranch. Too many things don't add up. His horses aren't targeted. He can't afford a security system like you offer. And the surveillance? He can't afford that. And, who was that in the Audi? An Audi for crying out loud. He doesn't have friends who drive Audis."

He rubbed his forehead. "Look, I'm not bound by any confidence here, so I don't think I'm giving anything away I'm not supposed to, but I think something is definitely going on here. What do you know about RRI?"

She rolled the letters RRI through her head as relief settled in her gut. "Nothing."

Mac glanced down the road then back to her, the short

hairs on the back of her neck tingled. "Let's jump in my truck."

As they climbed into his truck, he leaned forward and pulled his laptop case from the passenger floor, pulled his laptop from the case and opened it up. "Roberto Rocelli International."

He tapped a few keys and turned his computer so she could also see the screen. The information on RRI filled the screen, and she read the information he shared. Using the touchpad, she scrolled to the bottom of the page, then looked into his dark sparkling eyes. He opened a new browser window, and the information on Estefan Santos replaced the RRI information.

"That's the man in the Audi."

"Yes. I've seen him here before, in the house with Carlson. Then we found this." He pulled up another window, and the security cameras appeared in little boxes on the screen. He clicked on one and enlarged the feed. An open stall door showed stacked tan bags with RRI Grain Program in a stall. Someone entered the stall and hoisted a bag over his shoulder, the only thing visible on the man was a balding spot in the back of his head surrounded by light brown hair.

"What's the RRI grain program?"

"Haven't figured that part out yet." She could feel him watching her. She turned to face him, then without thinking she touched his face, running her thumb along his cheek. His head turned and kissed her palm, and her heart fluttered.

"About the investigation ..." He cleared his throat, and she started to interrupt him.

"Mac, it's ..."

"No, Stevie, let me explain." He reached forward and pulled a manila envelope from the glove compartment. He handed it to her; his lips turned down into a frown.

She looked at the envelope, and her heart raced as a flush raced up her chest, throat, and into her cheeks. She turned it over and saw it was sealed. Her eyes sought his. "It's not opened."

"No." His voice cracked. "I couldn't bring myself to open it."

She sucked in a deep breath. "So you don't know anything about me?"

He chuckled. "I didn't say that. I know you smell like peaches and it's tantalizing. I know how you feel when you're pressed against me and I love that. I know how you sound when I'm sliding into you, and it's sexy as hell. I know you love your family and that's endearing. I know you are good at your job and it makes me proud of you. I know you love a good drink of great bourbon, Evan's chicken, cute little shorts, and you love to laugh. All those things make me want to know more about you, but only if you want to tell me and only that way."

He nodded to the envelope. "Feel free to do what you want with that."

Wow.

She leaned up and kissed his lips, softly sliding hers along his, enjoying the taste of his mouth, the feel of his lips. She leaned her forehead against his and cupped her hand around his nape, holding him close. *American Soldier* by Toby Keith began playing.

He kissed her lips lightly, "Sorry." He pulled his phone from his pocket. "Dirks, what's up?"

He listened, then turned to his computer, clicked on the box showing the stall with the grain in it. He enlarged the box and saw that most of the grain had been moved. "Can you see where they're taking it?"

She leaned in and watched as the same man reached in for another bag, tossed it onto a cart, and then grabbed another.

Mac clicked again, and that window minimized. Another window appeared, and it showed the apron of the barn and no activity. She dipped her head to get a closer look and saw the cart piled with grain bags moving into the screen, out the back of the barn, and then out of sight of that camera. Clicking a few more times, another window appeared, and the man pushed the cart to a small building behind the barn.

"I'm on it. That's the grain barn. I wonder why they're moving it now? Hold on."

He tapped his phone. "Go ahead. I have you on speaker, and Detective Jorgenson is in the truck with me."

"Hello, Detective. So, here's the other thing, Evanston Carlson just made a significant deposit in the bank in town, the Depository."

"How significant?"

"Fifty thousand dollars."

Unable to control herself. "Where in the hell did he get fifty thousand dollars?"

She glanced at the ranch, the only part of it visible was the rooftops of the barn and the house. "Wait. Do you have any record of him selling any horses lately?"

Dirks could be heard tapping on a keyboard, then he responded. "No records in the registries. Depending on pedigree, it would have to be registered to command that price, correct?"

Calling on her horse knowledge, she was quick to respond. "Yes, depending on pedigree. A horse with no pedigree is basically a workhorse or a pleasure horse. They don't bring that kind of money."

"How about breeding records? Can you see any registrations in the breeding records that would link to Carlson?" Her heart pounded as pieces of the puzzle started coming together or at least sorting themselves out.

"No breeding records linked to Carlson. Would he use a different name?"

She lightly pursed her lips. "It's unlikely unless he's doing something illegal. Usually, when a ranch has secured a prime stallion, they love the prestige that goes with that. Believe me, these ranchers are all watching each other and seeing who is breeding with whom. Honestly, their coffee talk is all about which dam is covered by which stud." She smiled and looked into Mac's eyes.

20

His heart felt light, and the tension left his neck and shoulders. Despite the little episode of this morning, she was a reasonable person. Note to self, just give her some time when things get tough.

She asked, "How about doing a bigger search, Dirks? If he had a mare he was using as a surrogate for someone else, he might get a payment like that, depending on the sire. Can you search all records using Evanston Carlson and Whispering Caves Ranch?"

"Sure." Tapping sounded.

Hairs on the back of Mac's neck stood. Tension slid into his shoulders and unease settled in his gut. He twisted around in his truck looking down the road, behind them, and up into the tree-covered hills on both sides of the truck. Stevie glanced at him then mimicked his behavior as she slowly lifted her lacy loose fitting tank and pulled a pistol from the concealed belt she wore. She chambered a round and then retucked her pistol into its belt at her waist.

He shook his head slightly, and despite the tension that just filled the truck, he smiled. She was the perfect woman for him. Leaning low and reaching down to his ankle, he pulled his weapon from its holster, loaded a bullet into the chamber and slowly closed the lid on his laptop, never taking his eyes from the outside of the vehicle.

"Dirks? Something's not right here. If you start hearing things go down, get someone out here."

"Roger that."

Movement in the trees just outside his window caught his attention, but he didn't want to look and alert whoever was out there that he was on to them. Looking at Stevie, he nodded slightly. "Outside my window in the trees. See movement?"

She smiled and touched his face. "Yes."

He leaned forward and hugged her close. "What can you see?"

"Looks like two men. They're watching us."

He pulled away, lightly kissed her lips then stared into the crisp blue eyes that had first captivated him. "I'm going to pull up next to your Jeep. You get out of my truck and into your Jeep and get out of here."

"No."

"Stevie, I don't know what this is; please don't fight me on this."

"Jesus, Mac. I'm a detective with the Sheriff's Department; I can handle myself."

"I'm sure you can but ..."

"You did not just say that like you were placating a child."

"Shit." He started his truck. "Are they still watching?"

"Yes. I'm not driving away."

"Women."

"Listen, Mister ..."

Tapping on her window had them both turning to see a smaller, dark-haired man, dark brown eyes, bronze skin tapping on her window with his gun. He nodded as they both looked at him, then he motioned with his gun for them to exit the truck.

"Shit."

"Okay, listen, no quick movements." She turned toward the door then back to him and quickly said. "No heroics."

"You be careful." He slid his pistol from his lap and dropped it into the side pocket of cargos and turned to see the second man standing just outside of his window, a grin on his face.

He raised his hands in the air, and the man opened the truck door. Mac stepped from the vehicle, his heart in his throat, sweat beginning to slither down his back.

Once he was out of the truck the man standing before him jerked his chin toward the side of the road on the passenger side of the truck. He began walking, slowly, his mind racing, thoughts flying through his head so quickly he couldn't grasp them. This was a situation he'd never been in before.

As he neared the edge of the road, he chanced a glance at Stevie. Her jaw was clamped shut, her posture rigid, and her eyes were rounded. He could see her chest rising and falling; this was new territory for both of them.

The smaller of the two men pulled his cell phone from his pocket and tapped a couple of icons, held the phone to his ear and spoke. "We have them both."

Pocketing his phone, he looked at Stevie and pointed his gun at her chest. "Get on your knees."

She looked into his eyes and his gut twisted, but he nodded slightly.

"Don't look to him; he doesn't have the gun on you." The small man ground out.

She looked at him and slowly knelt down. The rage and fear rose in his chest; she shouldn't be kneeling before anyone. "Look, what do you want and what's this all about?"

Both men laughed, glancing between the two of them. A car pulled up behind his truck, and his heart raced, hope briefly rising in his chest that Dirks finally made it. But, he wouldn't just pull up to a scene like this, so his hopes were dashed as Estefan entered his peripheral vision then stood directly in front of him, gun pointed at his chest. Glancing at Stevie, her eyes narrowed on his, then he chuckled.

"Nice work getting the good detective here, Mac." Lowering his gun, he grinned.

His head jerked back as if he'd been slapped. He looked down at Stevie, and the the surprise in her face was unmistakable.

"So, Detective, let's have a little chat. Tell me what you think you know and then I'll decide what to do with you."

"Estefan, she doesn't know anything." His voice tightened and the look she landed on his threatened to freeze his heart.

"I want to hear it from her. Detective?"

"I don't know anything except Evie is mixed up in something, and clearly it has to do with you. But I'll figure it out. Then I'll bring you down," she spat out.

Estefan laughed. "She's a hot one, Mac. Temper, nice tits, full ass, and a smart mouth."

Mac raised his voice, "Stevie ..."

She glared up at him. "Don't. You. Dare."

Still laughing, Estefan continued. "Okay, so Mac, the boss wants to see you and congratulate you for a job well done, and these two, well they have a date with the good detective."

The two criminals chuckled as they turned their lascivious gazes to her.

21

She tried not thinking the worst but these two assholes were staring at her breasts like they couldn't wait to get their hands on them and her heart hurt if it was true and Mac had set her up.

"Peaches …"

"Don't." She looked him in the eye, the anger bubbling forward as Estefan tapped Mac on the shoulder then pointed his gun to Mac's truck.

"Okay. Peaches." The smaller man's sickening grin widened. "Let's go. Get on your feet and walk to the Jeep. Keep your hands where I can see em."

Rising slowly, she turned to her Jeep and walked to the driver's side. Things ran through her mind on how to alert someone of her dire situation. If she could just get a message to Tina, she'd be sure things would work out.

She heard Mac's truck door close, then her Jeep door on the passenger side opened, and her new companion slid into the passenger seat, gun trained on her. Her lacy tank now stuck to the skin on her back, her pink shorts which she'd proudly wore this morning now an irritant as they stuck to the damp skin on her legs. She dared not make a move to unstick her clothing. Opening her door, she slowly slid into the driver's seat, keys still in the ignition. She started the engine and waited for instructions. The partner to the little shithead next to her was in the Audi followed by Mac's truck. He looked straight ahead as he passed by and it made her stomach roll. She still could not get past the fact that he set her up. Didn't make sense – there'd be no reason for it.

"Follow your boyfriend, Detective," he sneered.

She swallowed and followed Mac's truck which promptly turned down the driveway to Whispering Caves. Her eyes roved the area for signs of anything that might help her to escape. It all seemed so normal, except the fact that Evie didn't employ very many people, and so the usual hustle and bustle of life on a ranch wasn't here. If Evie was going to decide her fate, she hoped he'd be grateful for the fact that in high school, she wasn't mean to him like the others. She just largely ignored him.

The Audi and Mac parked in front of the entry to the barn. She pulled alongside his truck not wanting to park him in, just in case they were able to get out of this some-how. Whatever this was.

Once they'd stopped and she'd put the Jeep in park, the sneering little shit alongside her nudged her with the tip of his gun. "Go on and follow your boyfriend, Detective."

"He's not my boyfriend."

The little imp laughed. "Yeah, right. Seems to me I saw you two hugging and kissing back there. Should have waited a bit longer to see what else you'd do. Anyway, looked like he was your boyfriend back there."

"That was before I knew he'd set me up."

He opened the door and twisted his head. "Never know I guess."

She opened her door and stepped from the Jeep. She'd had the air conditioning running on this short ride, it did help just a bit to keep her lacy loose-fitting tank from sticking to her. She didn't want her holster to show, it was quite possibly the only thing that might prove to save her life. Walking toward the barn, her heart hammered in her chest, and her throat became dry.

Three pairs of eyes turned toward her and her companion as they entered the barn. The cool air from the overhead fans helped to keep her from overheating. Her sweaty palms hadn't felt the light breeze just yet.

"Detective, it appears you've been lying to me." Estefan eyed her, a frown on his handsome face. Now that she thought about it, his recent behavior made him decidedly ugly now.

She lifted her chin and leveled her gaze on him. "About what?"

She flicked her eyes to Mac then back to Estefan. Her heart beat faster when she saw Mac staring at her. The barn doors burst open, and Evie walked into the barn, voice raised. "What the hell is going on out here?"

That was her chance. She kicked out at the man in front of her, connecting squarely with his groin. He doubled over in a heap, and as he was going down, she kneed him in the face, hearing the bone in his nose snap. It twisted her stomach for an instant, but the adrenaline kept her going. He raised his hands to his nose, and she took the opportunity to bend his hand back, snapping the finger inside the trigger and forcing him to cry out in further pain.

A gunshot rang out, and she quickly forced her back against Mac's. She glanced around and saw that he'd taken the same opportunity to disarm Estefan and his minion. Both of them were lying on the ground. Estefan had been shot, a small red dot at the base of his throat—his body lifeless. The minion was doubled over and moaning.

"Jesus, what the hell is going on here?" Evie's quivering voice once again caught her attention. He'd backed against a stall door, holding his hand over his heart, his eyes as big as silver dollars, his skin extremely pale.

At first, she held the gun in her hand toward him. As he slid down the wall, she lowered her weapon. Mac checked the pulse on Estefan, then stepped over him to the moaning men on the ground, and one by one checked them for weapons. He pulled them away from each other, then walked back to her where he pulled his phone from his pocket and swiped and tapped.

"Dirks, where are you?"

"I'm right here." Dirks appeared in the doorway, gun up, eyes alert and searching. As soon as he saw things were under control, he holstered his weapon and walked toward Mac.

She pulled her phone out and called the station, asking them to bring patrols and an ambulance. Pocketing her phone, she'd managed her breathing, and her shaking extremities began to calm. She vaguely listened as Mac relayed the scenario to Dirks and she walked to Evie and squatted down in front of him.

"What's going on here, Evie?" She was proud that her voice sounded remarkably calm and she patiently waited, something she didn't feel at all.

He cleared his throat, quickly glanced at the men lying on the apron floor and swallowed.

"They were paying me to test their feed. It's supposed to help my horses build muscle and stamina faster to get them stronger and faster to qualify for the racing season."

She pursed her lips as she studied his face. "What's in it?"

"Certain growth hormones, then something to hide it when testing."

She heaved out a breath. "Evie ..."

His voice raised. "You don't know what it's like. Your family has been revered in these parts. Your family was able to overcome the scandal that could have plagued it. Instead, it plagued me."

She stood and rubbed her fingers over the back of her neck. What the hell.

22

———

The past four days had been a whirlwind of activity, beginning with his being interviewed by the police about the shooting and the activities that revolved around it. RRI had been poisoning the area horses to see just how much Oleander it would take for them to get just sick enough that they couldn't race and how long that took effect. The point being they'd have it figured out by next year's Derby, and at the same time, strengthening Carlson's horses to fix the race and dominate the gambling surrounding the races.

Evie was ignorant of the poisonings; he just jumped for the quick, easy money. He'd do no jail time, but his horses were disqualified from competing next year. So once again, his family was launched into a scandal involving drugging of animals, though it was a bit different this time.

He'd tried calling Stevie a few times, but she never answered, and he never left a message. What would he say? I didn't set you up?" He didn't, and he was pissed off that she would think that. He felt like he'd been riding a roller coaster since he met her. But, tonight he was going to try and speak with her.

He pulled his truck up to the garage door of her apartment above the laundromat. He smiled when he thought of it. In searching for the landlord of this property to inquire about a doorbell system, he found that one Stephanie Jorgenson owned the building and was indeed the landlord. She owned the laundromat and four other rentals in town. She was growing into a real estate mogul.

He knocked on her door and turned the knob, finding it locked. He turned and leaned against the building, resting his head against the warm brick and breathing deeply of the fresh laundry scent surrounding him.

The door at the back of The Brass Rail opened, and her laugh floated across the parking lot to him. He pushed himself off the wall and sauntered to the bar. Entering the back hallway, her laugh grew louder as he moved into the pool area. There she was chatting with Schmoo, laughing at the redheaded woman wearing a headband with horse ears on it, some crazy bright red shorts and work boots. She sure could put a person in a good mood. His eyes landed on Stevie, and his heartbeat thundered down the racetrack. The woman was simply stunning. Her blonde hair captured the light, and the halo once again surrounded her. Her head thrown back in laughter, her perfect smile was a sight to behold. Her fabulous breasts jiggled slightly as she moved, the light blue button-up blouse showcased her cleavage and hugged her waist at the same time. She wore denim cutoffs and cowboy boots. Her perfect legs, tanned from the sun, were shapely and long. His fingers itched to touch her; his body came alive looking at her now.

He made his way toward her and stopped just in front of her. Schmoo giggled. "I'll get you a bourbon, Mac." And scooted off to get his drink.

His eyes feasted on hers for a few moments. "You shootin' pool?"

She smiled, her eyes caressing his face. "A buck and a drink."

"You're a sight to behold, Stevie. I've missed you this week. Tell me what's going on." He ran the backs of his fingers down her face enjoying the feel of her soft, warm skin against his. His eyes locked on hers. His hand finished its journey and slid behind her neck and into her hair. He leaned down and kissed her lips. Soft, warm, and supple, her lips kissed him back. Sliding his tongue along hers, the warmth of her mouth seeped into his, the hint of bourbon on her tongue brought back recent memories. The scent of peaches and cream surrounded him.

He stepped back, hating to do so, but wanting to make sure there were no doubts.

"It's been a long week, Mac. The investigation is somewhat complete now. My father's mare passed away, and I've had time to process everything in my head. I know you didn't set me up."

"I'm not that kind of man, Peaches."

"I know."

Schmoo brought his drink and set it on the table next to where they stood. Stevie smiled as she watched Schmoo walk away with her horse ear headband, and he took a moment to rack the balls for a game. He needed the distance to settle himself down. His hands shook, and his heart was trying to burst free of his chest.

The balls racked, he turned to see her watching him, her chest rising and falling rapidly—good news there. He stepped back and motioned for her to break the balls. Now that was a sight, her bent over the pool table, her rounded ass in those little cutoffs something he'd remember for years to come.

She walked toward him, stopped directly in front of him, placed her hand over his heart and locked eyes with him. "I'm in love with you, Sam McKenzie."

His heart raced, his breath whooshed from his lungs, and his fingers shook as he slid them into her soft blonde hair. "I'm in love with you, Stephanie Jorgenson."

He kissed her and held her tightly, absorbing this feeling he never wanted to lose.

Someone whistled from the bar, and he remembered where they were. He kissed the tip of her nose.

"So, Bluegrass Security was invited to the Race to the Derby party at the Murphy Equestrian Center this weekend to watch the Derby. I understand it's a big deal, barn dance and all. Would you be my date?"

Smiling, her perfect lips slightly moist and always sexy, she breathily responded, "I'd love to be your date."

Entering the Bluegrass Security office, Stevie waved to Regina. "Hey, Regina; what's up today?"

"Not too much, Stevie. A day like any other. Mac's upstairs."

Making her way to the stairs, it was impossible to contain the smile that crossed her lips as she now felt like this place was a second office to her. She and Mac had been seeing each other for just over two months now. Ammo had healed and was his old self, though that puzzle was still unsolved. Mac left him inside the house with his door closed when he wasn't around for a while. Ammo enjoyed his freedom of the door when they were home. That brought another smile to her face. Home. She spent more nights out at Fire Lake than she did at her apartment. She had helped him with the kitchen remodel, adding white cabinets, hardwood floors and granite counters, it was now a showpiece on a smaller scale but homey and beautiful. It was a fun project working together, and they'd enjoyed the process so much, next week they were starting on the master bathroom. She'd spent much of today looking at websites and getting ideas.

At the top of the stairs, she waved at the four employees manning computer monitors and walked to Mac and Dirks' office. Both men were sitting at their desks, each working away on their respective computers.

"Afternoon, gentlemen." She walked directly to Mac and smiled when he promptly stood and wrapped her in his arms.

"Hey, Stevie," Dirks replied.

"Afternoon, Peaches." He kissed her lips then bent down and turned off his computer. "We thought we'd head to the Brass Rail for a drink before heading home tonight. You up for that?"

"Sounds good."

He took her hand, and Dirks stood to follow them. They stopped in front of Levi and Sage's closed door; then Mac tapped twice then quickly opened it, a grin on his face. He stuck his head in the door. "We're heading out."

The door opened all the way, and Sage shoved Mac's shoulder and wrapped her in a hug. "Great to see you, Stevie." She giggled as if she had a secret, but took Levi's hand and walked to the steps.

Settling themselves at a tall table next to the half wall so they could watch the pool table, the group got their drinks. Chuck joined them just as they were served. Before drinking, Dirks said, "I want to propose a toast. To all who are with us, peace and love. To those who are no longer with us, we miss you. And here's to a bright future."

Glasses were tapped, and drinks were enjoyed. Mac leaned down to her ear and said, "You shootin'?"

Smiling into his face, she nodded. "A buck and a drink."

He grinned and went to rack the balls. Sage giggled and seemed oddly excited. Levi glanced at Sage and pulled her into his arms whispering in her ear.

Stevie trekked back to the cue rack and picked her favorite cue, walked to the pool table, and bent to break the balls and froze. There on top of the cue ball lay a perfect, stunning, glittering diamond ring. Tears stung her eyes, and she turned to see Mac on one knee. "Will you marry me, Stephanie Jorgenson?"

Staring into those deep brown eyes she'd fallen in love with, though slightly blurry now through her tears, her heart melted. Swallowing, she whispered, "Yes."

He scooped her into his arms, and she held on tight, the feel of him crushing her to him the best feeling in the world. He set her on her feet and kissed her fully. Every one of her senses absorbed this moment. The way he felt wrapped around her, the taste of his lips, the smell of his cologne, the warmth of his body, and the cheers of their friends. She turned and there stood Toni and Al, the smiles on their faces enormous. Sage giggled like a schoolgirl, and Chuck and Dirks were lining up shots.

Mac turned to their group of friends, and said, "She said yes."

Danger, Desire, and a Love Worth Fighting For

Chuck Layton is ready to prove he's got what it takes at Bluegrass Security, but his latest case is more complicated —and enticing—than he bargained for. A chance encounter with widowed salon owner Nita Brown turns his investigation into a race against time, as her troubled son becomes tangled in a dangerous web of secrets.

Nita's only goal has been to protect her son, but when the rugged rookie investigator steps into her life, sparks fly. As they work together to uncover the truth, their undeniable chemistry ignites into a passion neither expected.

Can Chuck and Nita solve the case and protect her son, or will this road of lethal love lead to heartbreak?

📚 Don't miss Lethal Love! Grab your copy now and feel the heat! 🔥 Get it here! https://geni.us/LethalLove

ENJOY THIS BOOK? YOU CAN MAKE A BIG DIFFERENCE

Your Review Matters!

As an independent author, I don't have the big budgets of major publishers for splashy ads or subway posters (not yet, anyway 🙂). But what I do have is something far more valuable—amazing readers like you.

Your honest review is one of the most powerful ways to help my books reach other readers. If you enjoyed this story, taking just a few minutes to share your thoughts would mean the world to me. Reviews, even short ones, make a huge difference.

Click below to leave your review and help others discover *Finish Line*:

➡️ https://geni.us/FinishLineBGS

Thank you for your support—it means everything! 🤍

MEET PJ

About the Author

Writing has always been my dream, but it wasn't until I found the courage to put pen to paper that my life changed in the most profound way. Creating stories that resonate with readers and bringing to life flawed yet lovable characters brings me endless joy—and I hope my books bring you the same.

When I'm not writing, you'll likely find me enjoying time with my family or hitting the open road with my husband, Gene. We're avid bikers who love exploring new destinations, meeting fascinating people, and soaking in the beauty of this incredible country.

Coming from a proud family of veterans—including my grandfather, father, brother, two sons, and daughter-in-law—I have a deep appreciation for service and the sacrifices that protect our freedoms. Their dedication inspires me every day, and I'm honored to share stories that celebrate resilience, love, and the American spirit.

My online home is https://www.pjfiala.com.
You can connect with me on Facebook at https://www.facebook.com/PJFialaı,

and
Instagram at https://www.Instagram.com/PJFiala.
If you prefer to email, go ahead, I'll respond - pjfiala@
pjfiala.com.